CHRISTMAS AT FIRST SIGHT

Trevor McCall

CHAPTER ONE

Mrs. Dalloway said she would buy the flowers herself.

Paige Langford recited the opening words from her favorite novel out loud to make it a physical reminder of the uncomfortable conversation she needed to have that evening with Jessica. The sentence had become a mantra of personal responsibility to her during the nearly two decades that had passed since she first read it. The fact that no one was in the car to hear her speak confirmed an equally as old habit she had of amusing herself with personal jokes. She liked making herself laugh.

Paige parked her late-model BMW behind the equally ostentatious late-model Mercedes that belonged to her podcast producer and co-creator, Jessica. She was the same Jessica who inspired the flower-purchasing reminder, by way of Mrs. Dalloway. Of course, neither woman cared about the cars they drove as much as the brand names suggested. They both considered exotic car buying a necessary concession to living in Los Angeles and working in the entertainment industry. The city had a way of forcing a person to sacrifice core values for the sake of appearances.

Unfortunately for Paige, the longer she stayed, the more core values she escorted to the altar. Making these sacrifices was not something she enjoyed. It hurt her opinion of herself that she could not point to a specific moment in her history where they began to occur. One day, she was an idealistic aspiring young author fresh out of college. The next she was thirty-five, driving around in a late-model German sports car and writing half-hour television shows for an up and coming streaming network.

The self-published series of young adult novels she wrote over the last seven years was her consolation prize. The series was called Broken Vessels. It was about a girl who had been cursed to travel through time by a character from Chaucer's Pardoner's Tale. All four novels had done well, in self-publishing terms, but she still felt something lacked in her life. She never could put her finger on what that thing was. She also felt that the podcast she did with Jessica made her happy. Most of the time. Today was a different story.

Her modest, structurally sound, pleasantly appointed tiny house, only had enough space in the driveway for one and a half cars. This meant that half of Paige's BMW protruded into her minuscule front lawn. Under ordinary circumstances, this wouldn't be a problem. However, Paige's neighbor, Mr. Wyatt, was retired. He moved in less than three months ago, after leaving a job on the East Coast. He obsessed over the quality and quantity of grass that grew in and around his yard. Paige knew she would hear some convoluted metaphor from him in the morning. It would be a long-winded, ineptly camouflaged rebuke for killing her own grass. He might not even wait until the morning to deliver it. Sometimes he came over after eating dinner.

His favorite analogy was to compare her parking on her own yard to men who wore baseball hats for decades. The reason this was so bad was never directly spelled out. This left Paige to infer Mr. Wyatt equated male pattern baldness with wearing baseball hats. Paige imagined some doctor once explained Mr. Wyatt's own vanishing hairline with the hat hypothesis. She further imagined the concept struck a nerve with Mr. Wyatt, based on the number of times he brought it up to her while he cited her for yard malfeasance.

Paige switched her car off and sat for a moment in the unseasonably warm early December night air. It had been over a week since she and Jessica had delivered their now infamous Five Things I Hate About Christmas podcast. Their show had always been moderately successful, but the Anti-Christmas episode was their biggest ratings bonanza in the two years that they had recorded material. They allowed themselves to believe it set them up for the bigger things they both talked about when they began their podcasting journey together. Jessica wanted to become a television and film director. Paige wanted to write The Next Great American Novel. This fake title was another of her jokes with herself. Her imaginary book would have to be called The Next Great American Novel because Philip Roth wrote The Great American Novel way back in 1973. She wanted to one-up the legend and beat him at his own name game.

She sat in her car in the heat because she knew what awaited her when she entered her house. Jessica would immediately begin trying to convince her to accept the modest proposal from Vincent Turner, first resident of Dayton, New Hampshire. On behalf of the 1,607 people who also called the small town on the Western Shore of Lake Winnipesaukee home, he had invited Paige and Jessica to 'come do Christmas in New Hampshire'. The town would pay to fly them there and put them up for free in the village's five-star bed-and-breakfast.

Of course, the catch was that Paige and Jessica would do their show in Dayton during the run-up to Christmas. Instead of doing one episode per week like they normally did, they would do an episode each day they were there. It would all lead up to a special, live, Christmas Eve podcast. Mr. Turner obviously believed the free advertising provided by Paige's extremely popular internet-based show would more than make up for the couple of thousand dollars the town would spend on bringing Paige and Jessica from Los Angeles to New Hampshire. Paige sighed. If that had been the only catch in Mr. Turner's plan, she would have already agreed to his terms.

Paige grabbed her small attaché case and purse from the front seat and exited her car. As she approached her front door, she cast furtive glances toward Mr. Wyatt's dining-room window. She worried she would see him standing there, pointing at his receding hairline while making pressing motions with his other hand at her yard. Somehow, her luck held. He wasn't in the window judging her. She managed to gain entry to her house without enduring another upbraiding from the grass-loving Mr. Wyatt. Paige hoped this was a positive omen for the talk she had to have with her co-creator.

Jessica greeted her from the dining room, where their equipment remained set up year-round. "Hey, girl. How was your workday?"

"Last one before winter break, so it couldn't be

all bad." Paige set her attaché case and purse down on the couch as she walked past it. "How was yours?" She entered her small dining room and gave Jessica a warm hug.

"Same old, same old. Your food's in the microwave." Jessica fiddled with the microphone controls —unnecessarily, as far as Paige could tell. It was typical of her, always needing her hands on every part of production, even when nothing needed adjusting.

"Thanks, I'm starving." Paige headed toward the kitchen. "What did you get us this time?"

"China One," Jessica replied.

"The one on Melrose?" Paige opened the door of her microwave and removed the takeout.

"Is there another one?" Jessica asked.

Paige fought her literal side. She succeeded in not saying there were three other China One locations within a five-mile radius of her house. Paige knew the one on Melrose was the only one that was consistently good. Of course, Paige also knew this was what Jessica meant by asking if there was another one. She wondered if her impulse to be contrary toward Jessica was a result of the discussion she was about to have with her over Mr. Turner's New Hampshire offer. She decided to bring it up first in an effort to control the narrative. "So, I've been thinking about Mr. Turner's offer."

Jessica didn't push. Paige knew that move well— the quiet space, the way Jessica let her steer, until the outcome felt like Paige's idea. Her eyes gave it away, bright with calculation she never voiced. Paige had seen that look during pitch meetings and scheduling fights.

She was playing the long game. "Oh yeah?" Jessica asked almost innocently.

"Yeah." Paige came into the dining room with the Chinese food Jessica picked up for her. She sat down across from her and began to eat.

"And?"

Paige was going to make Jessica wait as long as possible for her decision. She considered taking another bite just to draw it out a moment longer. Love for Jessica got the better of her. "It's a good offer." Paige replied with no trace of commitment in her voice.

"We've established it's a good offer. How many people get paid to take a Christmas vacation?" Jessica formed her right palm into the shape of a zero, thereby answering her own question.

"It's just that... I don't think... I don't feel like I want to do it." Paige knew she had left herself wide open to counterattack with that waffling response. What was wrong with her? Jessica would notice the indecisive phrasing. She would pounce on the opportunity it presented her.

Of course, Jessica proved Paige's intuition correct by leaping on the opportunity. "Well, if you aren't sure either way, we should just do it."

Paige focused on trying to grip a piece of sweet and sour chicken with the complimentary pair of chopsticks that came with every meal from China One. As was usual for her and this endeavor, she made no headway. She finally gave up and used the 'just in case' fork she had brought with her to the table. "That seems like a wildly inaccurate representation of what I actually said."

Jessica abandoned subtlety. Paige clocked the shift instantly—no more nudging, no more soft power. This was fire and argument, the tone Jessica saved for producers and legal teams, not her co-host. "Did you," she said, eyes sharp, "or did you not deliver the final draft of your show's last filmed episode before you left the studio today?" Paige had. Of course she had. That was the whole point. Jessica wasn't asking; she was cornering—and Paige knew it.

Paige sighed. She knew where this was going. "I did."

"Is, therefore, your show officially on Christmas break—at least as far as you writers are concerned?"

"It is." Paige completed the admission with another sigh.

Jessica leaned in like she'd just slipped on a prosecutor's badge. Paige could see the theater in it—the straightened spine, the deliberate cadence, the glint in her eye that meant she was about to ask something ruinous. "Do you," she said, "have a boyfriend in the greater Los Angeles area?"

Paige shook her head. "No."

"Fiancé?"

Paige was confused. "If I don't have..."

Jessica tossed meaning aside. Paige heard it in her tone—that sly abandon, the way every word was chosen less for truth than for effect. She was having fun now. Theater fun. "Husband?" Jessica asked with mock solemnity.

Paige laughed in spite of herself. "Now you're just

being silly."

Jessica shifted, posture composed like she'd been waiting to deliver the final line of closing arguments. Paige braced. "Remind me," Jessica said, smooth as glass, "what Mom and Dad are doing this Christmas?"

Paige narrowed her eyes as she looked at Jessica. She was trying to gauge the intent behind Jessica's comment. "*Bob* and *Glenda* are taking the trip to Europe they never got around to when *their* kids were young."

Jessica paused, distracted by the return of first names. "Why are we back to calling them Bob and Glenda?"

Paige glanced over, not expecting the detour. Jessica's frown wasn't sharp—just concerned, soft at the edges. She loved Paige. That much was never in question. But sometimes love meant watching her drift into abstraction, naming their parents like characters, sacrificing real connection for the purity of an idea. Jessica saw it happen. She always saw it happen.

"You know why I started doing that again, Jessica," Paige replied.

"I know why you did it when we were six," Jessica said, voice low. "But I don't know why it's back now. Thirty years is way beyond late for making changes to the script."

Paige didn't answer right away. Jessica's demeanor had shifted. She was less co-host, and a lot more sister. Whatever push she'd planned about New Hampshire was paused, suspended by something quieter. Jessica wasn't strategizing anymore. She was trying to keep Paige from making it worse. For Bob. For Glenda. For all of them.

"The reason I did it when I was six, is the same

reason I do it now that I'm thirty-five." Paige didn't want to fight with Jessica. She hoped that if she changed the subject, it would lighten the mood. She went with an easy choice. Making fun of one's age, that was always good for a splash of goodwill. "Thanks for reminding me exactly how ancient I am, by the way."

Jessica smiled. She seemed to consent to Paige's desire to move the topic under discussion away from the reasons why Paige wouldn't refer to Bob and Glenda as Mom and Dad by joining in on Paige's joke. "It's exactly how ancient I am too you know." She then summed up her previous point with what Paige took to be a bright-red, very Christmassy looking, entirely rhetorical bow. "Anyway, since Bob and Glenda are out of town, and you have no one keeping you here. What is it you think justifies our not making this trip?"

Paige grimaced. Her ploy to change the subject partially backfired. Paige realized her recently adopted reason for calling her Mom and Dad by their given names was almost identical to the reason she found herself uninspired by Christmas. The epiphany, while enlightening, was not pleasant. "I'm sorry, Jessica. I just feel so strongly that this is something I shouldn't do." Paige waited to see if this was going to be enough of a reason. When Jessica remained silent, Paige plowed ahead. "Because it wouldn't be real. I can't pretend to believe in things I know don't exist."

Jessica's face twisted into something close to delight. Her sarcasm was in full bloom. Paige felt it before the words landed. "I agree," Jessica let a small silence fill the air. Paige knew she felt she was about to deliver her sharpest barb yet. "It wouldn't be real." Paige frowned.

Jessica's logic was closing in on irrefutable. "Because that television show you write—it's based on a true story, right? The four time-travel novels on Amazon, the half-finished literary one you've got holed up in your laptop... those are all gospel truths, right?"

Paige didn't blink. She just stared. They both knew how much water the excuse could carry. Not a drop. Jessica's insistence on fighting her so hard exasperated Paige. She began to wonder if this New Hampshire trip was going to turn into one of those things that drove a wedge between people. "You know what I mean, Jessica. The TV show and the book are different from the podcast." Paige pointed at the recording equipment on her dining room table. "This is more like journalism, or personal essays. People expect this to be real."

Paige watched as Jessica recalibrated. "You know how close we are," she said, gently this time. "How hard we've worked to build this audience. We're holding a winning hand, and you want to fold." Paige didn't look away. "That Five Things episode? We may never hit like that again. What if podcasts die in two months? All podcasts—not just ours." Paige's jaw tightened. Jessica saw it. Paige was close to tipping. Jessica saw it, and reached for the one card that always pierced Paige's armor. "Are you afraid?" she asked, "of having money and a room of your own?"

Paige smiled. Another beautiful line from the author of her flower-buying-mantra. The quote moved Paige over the edge. She knew Jessica would keep pushing her advantage until she submitted. "All right, Jessica. You win. Although I request it be noted in the permanent record that your Virginia Woolf quotation was a low blow."

"I won fair and square," Jessica said, too quickly. Paige caught the edge in her tone—not triumph, exactly, but the need to be believed. Jessica wasn't gloating. She was guarding something deeper. She didn't want the win tainted, didn't want Paige to flinch or twist it into manipulation. This mattered. Paige knew that. Jessica needed the victory to mean something clean.

"You know how much I adore Virginia Woolf for defining the boundaries of being a female writer. Please be advised I reserve the right to win one argument between us before Christmas just by saying the name Virginia Woolf." Paige stared Jessica down just to let her know she was serious. If they had a disagreement at any time within the next few months, Paige expected Jessica to let her have *her* way.

Jessica considered the offer. "Those are the conditions of your surrender?"

Paige laughed. "They are."

"Agreed." Jessica looked at Paige with some concern showing on her face. "Now that we've settled what we're doing for Christmas, any idea what we do for this show we are supposed to record tonight?"

"Jessica Keller, I believe you are worried." Paige enjoyed the fact Jessica was anxious about the show. She considered it a tiny bit of reward for all Jessica put her through by insisting they take their show to New Hampshire.

It wasn't that Jessica was twisting her arm and making her fly to New Hampshire. It had more to do with Paige knowing Jessica needed the podcast to take them to the next level way more than Paige did. It was true that with a highly successful podcast under her belt, one that had a built-in audience she could pitch to at least once a week, any book Paige completed would get her a respectable publishing contract. Jessica had made this argument to Paige more than a few times since the Anti-Christmas podcast aired.

Of course, it was also true Paige already had an agent who was willing to read her books and submit them to publishers as soon as they were finished. On top of this, she knew how to market herself to sell books in the digital expanse dominated by Amazon. The real reward, Paige felt, was in sheltering Jessica from the fact the podcast didn't need her camera production abilities in a rigorously necessary kind of way. In other words, Paige could live without Jessica, but Jessica would be pressed to make it in the world of content creation entertainment without Paige.

Jessica knew these facts too, at least in outline form. What Jessica did not know was that Paige had turned down multiple, escalating offers for the podcast. A streaming service that was a rival to her native network contacted her through her television agent and offered a substantial sum to turn the backlog of podcasts into a series of half-hour dramedies with an up-and-coming comedienne in the 'Paige' lead. The problem was they just wanted Paige. They weren't prepared to extend their generosity to Jessica as well. Of course, Paige would never try and soak up all the money. She would split the money with Jessica fifty-fifty no matter what happened. It was just that the people who contacted her were unwilling to include Jessica as a creative member of the television show's production team.

Paige knew that Jessica was far more interested in credit than cash. A deal that gave her a tiny bit of financial freedom would be a godsend. However, Paige was certain any such deal would be dead on arrival at Jessica's doorstep because Jessica wanted a career as a producer, not a payday. She would never be willing to be The Omission from the future of the show she helped to launch. It would be too damaging to her opinion of herself for Paige to tolerate, or risk. For this reason, Paige rejected the increasing purchase terms without ever letting Jessica know offers had even been fielded. Why upset her with the knowledge she had basically become an afterthought on her own program?

Paige directed her attention away from the thoughts she was having about Jessica's future levels of professional embarrassment and dove headfirst back into the idea Jessica was nervous about Paige not preparing written material for the show. "Let me ask the question more directly. Are you worried, Ms. Keller?"

After a moment of intense concentration, Jessica admitted that the sour look on her face was caused by worry. "Well, I know how mercurial you writer-types can be. I was afraid you hadn't put anything together for tonight's show and we might have to make it up as we go. You know how much I hate those wing-it episodes."

Paige turned sideways in her chair. She picked up two stacks of paper from the hutch, which sat behind her. She placed them on the table in front of Jessica. The stack of papers on Jessica's left-hand side said, Christmas in New Hampshire. The stack of papers on her right-hand side said, Christmas in Los Angeles. "I'm a writer, Jessica; I never want to show my Rough Drafts unless I have one heck of a good reason."

Jessica smiled, head tilted just slightly. Paige had slipped the name of their show into their conversation with surgical precision—never once needing to say it aloud. It was the kind of thing Jessica admired and never tried to imitate. Broad strokes were her domain. Paige had always been the last-idea genius, the one who could thread meaning where others lost the needle. Jessica never seemed bitter about it. If anything, she wore it like armor—proud of her eye for talent, content to curate rather than create. Paige had heard her say it before: know your lot in life and live it fully. "Did I say mercurial?" Jessica asked, still smiling. "I meant brilliant."

"Give my mercurial, and brilliant, self, another minute to finish this food you brought. Then we'll do a read-through of what I have prepared. See if there are any areas you want to expand on..."

Jessica interrupted with a dart to the heart of Paige's former objection to taking the trip. "You mean you want me to practice... making it real."

"You've made your point and gotten your way. Is there anything else you need from me?" Paige thought about stamping her foot to show she meant business.

"Can you rename the main character in your Important Book after me? I don't think there's ever been a Jessica in one of those Virginia Woolf-type books. I want to be the first." Paige pierced Jessica with a look of effervescent disdain. Jessica returned Paige's gaze back to her with a double-shot of studied nonchalance. "What?" she asked.

"You are impossible." Paige stood up and walked

the twenty or so feet from her dining room to her kitchen. She rinsed the fork and threw the takeout container into the trashcan, which lived under the sink.

"Just don't forget I was impossible before you were famous. Or, at least, I was really, really difficult." Paige smiled, letting the words sink in. Jessica said it like a punchline, but Paige knew better. They'd weathered every version of themselves—six years old to high school, split campuses, long stretches of silence followed by phone calls that started mid-sentence. Thirty years, give or take. And still, somehow, as close as two kids waiting for their turn at the gym water fountain, their shoes squeaking against polished floors.

"How could I forget, when you remind me every day?" Paige said, just as the doorbell rang.

"You expecting company?" Jessica asked.

"No," Paige replied. "I hope it's not another one of those people giving out free magazine subscriptions. The last one that came by tried to pretend like he was in high school and doing it to fund some trip to Europe. It was gross and I'm not in the mood." Paige went to her front door. She put her eye up to the peephole. "Oh, thank God. It's Mr. Wyatt."

"Thank God?" Jessica tilted her head. "For what?" Paige didn't take the bait. Jessica filled the quiet herself. "Well, at least it's bound to be a fun visit." The sarcasm landed clean. Icy, practiced, familiar… vintage Jessica. Whatever either of them expected from Mr. Wyatt's arrival, both knew it wouldn't entail divine gratitude.

Paige opened the door for Mr. Wyatt, but she did not move to the side in the way that was customary when you were about to welcome someone into your home.

"Good evening, Mr. Wyatt."

"Good evening, Paige. And please—I insist you start calling me Henry." Paige didn't respond. He handed her a plastic container, nudging it forward like a peace offering. "These are some muffins." Still nothing from Paige. "I... uh..." Henry faltered. The muffins were the excuse, not the point. He'd peeled them from a cardboard tray, tucked them into Tupperware to make them look homemade—or at least neighborly. He waited for her to take them, to save him from explaining. No such luck. "Had these," he muttered. "And I... uh... thought you might want some too."

Mr. Wyatt paused—ten full seconds—willing Paige to say something, anything, to let him off the hook. She didn't. Charity, she saw him finally realize, wasn't on offer tonight. "Right. Well, there it is." He nudged the container forward again. "I didn't want them anyway. Just thought you might." Another pause. This one was even longer. Paige persisted in her deafening silence. She knew he wasn't built for those. He was rapidly proving her correct. "I, uh... guess I'll head back now."

Mr. Wyatt took several steps away from Paige's door. However, his compulsion would not let him be. She knew he didn't want to have to admit to himself later he had come all the way over here, to her house, with the store-bought muffins he was trying to pass off as homemade, and not have said at least one of the things he wanted to say. He turned and faced Paige from her sidewalk. He removed his baseball hat and dabbed at his receding hairline with the palm of his left hand. "I don't know if I've told you this before or not, Paige, but parking on the yard like that is going to wear the grass all the way down to the mud."

"You have mentioned it, Mr. Wyatt." Paige smiled to let him know she didn't have any hard feelings toward him. He was a nice, retired, old man who would probably feed her cats for her when she went to New Hampshire. If she asked, which she wouldn't. And if she had any cats, which she didn't. She wasn't going to give him the satisfaction of being called Henry, even though her writer's instincts told her it would be symbolically appropriate somehow if she did. He could earn that little courtesy by ceasing to bother her about how she treated the grass in her yard. Why she thought it would be appropriate to call him by his first name was a literary mystery, she didn't have time to solve.

"Maybe I have mentioned that," Mr. Wyatt said. He hesitated, fingers tightening around the rim of his hat like it held the rest of the sentence. She knew what came next. Of course he'd said it before. Of course they both remembered. She knew he would be unable to resist. Again, she was proved correct. "It's a lot like what happens to men who wear a baseball cap too often. Especially if they get started with the habit when they're young."

"You've mentioned that before too, Mr. Wyatt." Paige wondered if the compulsive tendency which forced him to care about other people's lawns came before, or after, the compulsive tendency which forced him to tell the baseball hat analogy as soon as he finished critiquing parking abilities. How many habits did Mr. Wyatt have that were compulsive? More importantly, why did she find him endearing despite these habits? Jessica was also right. The magazine subscription people should be preferable to this annoying, old balding man. So, why weren't they?

"Have a good night, Paige."

"You too, Mr. Wyatt." Paige moved to shut the door. Mr. Wyatt stopped her. It was possible he had a small tear in his right eye. It was probably the heat, or an allergy.

"Paige?" Mr. Wyatt studied the ground as though it held the key to an important lock.

"Yes, Mr. Wyatt?" What other rule of yard management could she be breaking?

Mr. Wyatt opened his mouth several times. No sound came out. He swayed from side to side as though attempting to force his body to release the words which rattled around inside him. After several fits and starts that would later embarrass him for decades when he thought back on them, he gave up. "It's just that where I'm from, people are always looking for ways to help their neighbors out." When Paige didn't respond to this additional criticism, Mr. Wyatt tipped his cap to her, said, "Have a good night," then turned, and left Paige's porch. A departure that was as awkward as his arrival.

Paige shut the door with puzzlement brewing on her face. She rejoined Jessica in the dining room. "Want a blueberry muffin?" she asked as she popped the top off the Tupperware and took one for herself.

Jessica weighed the idea. "Sure, why not." She picked up one of the muffins and took a bite out of it. "Don't you get tired of that?"

"Oh, I don't mind, I guess. It's a little annoying, but it helps knowing he's vigilant about the properties. It's like having a one-man neighborhood watch." Paige was good at seeing the bright-side of things and people. Plus, it would be hard to explain the odd sort of tolerance she felt for Mr. Wyatt. It veered toward the magical side, and Paige didn't believe in things that didn't have concise explanations.

"Yeah, if you're a blade of grass, you're in good hands. Who knows if you're a human?" Jessica looked at the muffin in her hands. "Also, you know these aren't homemade, right? I mean, they're not bad. But it's a little weird to put store-bought muffins into a Tupperware container and bring them over to your neighbor's house to chastise her in an allegorical way about how she parks in her own driveway." Paige intuited Jessica had one more thing she wanted to say on the subject of Mr. Wyatt. "Didn't you feel like he was getting a little weird there at the end? I mean, you never know about people these days. What did his comment about the people where he's from mean? It felt cryptic to me."

"When you put it like that, maybe there was something weird to it." Paige shrugged her shoulders. She trusted her assessment of his personality. "I think he's harmless, though. It almost looked like he wanted to give me another tip, to be honest with you. Probably some other lawn and garden thing that really bothers him that I don't do." Paige dismissed Mr. Wyatt, his weirdness, and his complaints with a wave of her hand. Neither of them had time to spend on deciphering Mr. Wyatt. "Listen, Jess, I'm going to my bedroom to log into my computer and catch up on emails while you take a few minutes to review the pages." Paige fixed Jessica in a stare that wasn't entirely innocent. "It'll give you a chance to practice making it real for later, when we're recording."

To promote Jessica's engrossment in the reading, Paige left the dining room without waiting for her to reply. She entered her room and shut the door behind her. Paige always made sure to shut the door behind her because she never could let her guard down if there were a chance someone might happen by and see her. It was how she was wired. She exhaled deeply to let the stress of agreeing to the New Hampshire Christmas trip she didn't want to take, ebb. She then sat down in the chair that guarded the space in front of her desktop monitor and switched on the computer.

The icons stared out at her from a background picture of a woman sitting in a chair reading an open book. Beneath the picture were the words A Room of One's Own. Beneath that, in slightly smaller type, the author's name appeared—Virginia Woolf. Jessica's taunts were well aimed. Paige had a Virginia Woolf complex. Jessica would have been shocked to know that one of the root causes of this fascination was Paige's fear of never being able to write anything of substance. In other words, Paige knew she could write. That fact was clear to her in the four novels she had already written, and the episodes of the weekly streaming show she helped to crank out. What she lacked knowledge of, the thing she could not see clearly, was whether she could write *well*.

Paige extracted herself from the rabbit hole of thoughts about her own verbal competency. If she allowed too much thinking in that vein, she wouldn't get another thing done all night. In order to prevent that from happening, she distracted herself by clicking on the browser icon. When the search pane came up, she hovered over the upper right-hand side, on the 'accounts' button. Two showed up. One was in her name, Paige Langford. The other was in the name of the podcast she shared with Jessica, Rough Drafts. Paige clicked on the account for the podcast. The email for the show opened. There were 57 new emails.

Paige felt an author's exhilaration. Jessica never understood this part of the show. She advocated it was time to stop advertising their email address. For Paige, though, they weren't a burden. Sure, there might come a day when the time required to adequately answer all her emails eclipsed the amount of time she was prepared to spend on the activity. But that time had not yet arrived. She loved that people thought enough of the experiences she detailed on the podcast to send her an email. Jessica thought that the show's popularity was nearing a tipping point. Paige believed the tipping point was still a decent trek out into the future. If it ever did get to be too much, though, she thought their fans would understand because Paige would handle the situation openly. She also believed people responded best to honesty.

That last thought made her feel horrible. There was no way she could convince herself she was being honest with anybody by going to New Hampshire this Christmas. The New Hampshire plan was the opposite of honest. She shouldn't have told Jessica she would do it because there was no backing out now. Not that she imagined anyone would find out about the dishonesty. Only two people besides herself would know. One of those two people, Jessica, had been by Paige's side since they were six years old. There was no way she would ever let Paige down. The other person, Mr. Turner, was the mayor of Dayton. It would not be in his electoral best interests to divulge the secret either. And if Paige knew anything about local politicians, it was that they lived to be elected to office. If word got out that he participated in a scheme with Paige and Jessica, his election to another office within his county and state would be jeopardized. This meant it all boiled down to Paige. Was she strong enough to keep her own secret?

Paige laughed at herself as she flipped through the emails from the fans of her show. Of course, she was the one she could put the least trust in to keep her secret. How perfect was that? Her amusement turned cold when she pulled up a new batch of unread emails from the depths of her inbox. It was forwarded to her from her agent. She could see her agent had received the email from Adeline Press.

Paige did what she felt needed to be done. She deleted it without reading it. She didn't want to see an increase in the offer, or other more generous terms being offered to *her*, to the exclusion of Jessica. Annoyance bloomed in Paige. She directed it at her agent because she kept forwarding her these emails. She had told her agent, unequivocally, that she would not be accepting any deals for the show that didn't include a creative position for Jessica. What was so hard to understand about that?

Today's email showed her agent was now intent on forwarding the offers for the show to the email account of the show. Her agent probably didn't know this, but the email account for the show was an account Jessica often accessed. It was only a matter of time before Paige's other secret got out. She didn't have a plan for how to deal with Jessica's hurt feelings when it happened. It would be a dual-headed hydra too. Jessica would have to accept that her input wasn't valued by the people that wanted to buy the show and, at the same time, she would be forced to accept that Paige made the decision not to sell without consulting her. No matter how Paige tried slicing this particularly unappetizing collection of humble pie, all the sour parts kept ending up on Jessica's plate.

To protect herself from feeling guilty, Paige searched her email for the original correspondence from Mr. Turner, the mayor of the town of Dayton. Once found, she opened it and dashed off a quick reply. She said that she and her co-creator would be accepting his offer to visit New Hampshire, if that offer were still open. She included in her response that they would be accepting all the terms Mr. Turner demanded. She added emphasis to the text so that Mr. Turner would know the deal was for everything. Paige was even agreeing to the terms she found dishonest.

Paige then closed the lid on her laptop with a dramatic flair that wasn't customary for her. She had decided. They were taking their show to New Hampshire. Paige hoped this wouldn't become one of those defining moments in her life, but something told her it would turn out that way. Paige had never sold out before. Part of the reason her novels were self-published instead of traditionally published was because she refused to authorize the changes to make the story 'more commercial' that the publishing houses wanted. Paige didn't delude herself into thinking her young adult stories were literature, but they were her stories the way she wrote them. Unhappy endings and all.

These thoughts about her integrity left her hoping that when she and Jessica talked about this experience twenty years from now, it would warm their hearts. Paige hated to think she would go to all this trouble, destroy so much of what was dear to her, just to help Jessica, if it didn't end up being significant to her.

CHAPTER TWO

Eli Ryder sat at the only table in the one-room waiting area at the Laconia Regional Airport anxiously awaiting the two women who had been scheduled to arrive at 11:30 that morning. The mayor, Vincent, couldn't pick them up because of a prior engagement. Since the podcasters would be staying at Eli's bed-and-breakfast anyway, Vincent asked Eli to 'do him a solid'—those were the mayor's words—and represent the town at the airport. Because Eli's daughter, Lucy, would be in school until 3:30 in the afternoon, Eli agreed. Now that it was almost 1 o'clock and there was no sign of the podcasters from LA, he wished he hadn't.

He sat in the lounge chair doing simple arithmetic in his head. The longest he could imagine it taking to get home from the airport was an hour and a half. This implied that if he and his big-city charges were on the road by 1:30, he would be home in time to meet Lucy at the bus stop. Still, Eli was an extra-cautious parent. A lot of people would say he was too extra-cautious. Part of him wanted to prove that 'too extra cautious' assessment wrong by waiting until 1:30 to make any moves to cover the bus stop. However, a much bigger part of him wanted to be sure nothing concerning his daughter was ever left to chance.

Toward that 'too extra cautious' end, he called his best friend, Ian Parrish, to see if he could be at the bus stop in Eli's stead if something did go wrong. Ian was the generalized handyman for Eli's bed-and-breakfast. In every way but the official one, he was more co-manager with Eli than Eli's generalized handyman. Ian didn't know it yet, but after Christmas he would be officially promoted to co-manager. Eli had decided over Thanksgiving dinner to take Ian on as a partner.

Ian answered Eli's call on the third ring. He immediately agreed to be at the bus stop to meet Lucy. After a brief conversation about the building supplies they needed for a repair to the newest cabin on the property, Eli hung up feeling infinitely less anxious. As he sat at the table, the stress ran from his body the way a difficult child runs from his parents in a crowded store, with abandon. In the hours he had waited for the plane, he had spiked himself up into a knot of worry. He hadn't noticed how bad it had gotten until the moment when Ian agreed to drop everything in his life and go to the bus stop on Eli's behalf. It wasn't until the basin of his anxiety began to drain that he noticed how full it had become.

Anna had been the first person to accuse him of being a 'helicopter' parent. It would be a significant understatement to put it so plainly, but that aspect of his personality hadn't gotten any better in the four years since her death. Eli found it hard to accept the fact that there were things in life that could harm the ones he loved even if he did his utmost to protect them. His subconscious mind still hadn't accepted it. Anna's absence was more of a thing that happened in a movie about his life than something that was literally part of his chronology, despite the passage of those four years without her.

The trait of overcompensating on the side of protection had always been present in him. After the illness took Anna from him and Lucy, that trait amplified. He knew he had to loosen up at some point, or Lucy would run as far away from him as she could get when she became a teenager. He planned to respect her need for independence when it manifested. But if his own experience was any indication, that yearning for independence was still two years, or more, away. He was sure he had time.

Thinking of Anna reminded him how the idea for the bed-and-breakfast was hers. When they found out they would be having Lucy in the months after they graduated from the University of Virginia with dual master's degrees in education, she insisted they move to New Hampshire. Her family lived there. They would be able to help with the baby while she and Eli saved money to start their own business. He never questioned the switch from education to business that happened in Anna after the pregnancy. As far as Anna was concerned, Eli considered himself lucky to be along for the ride. She didn't have to love him.

Still, their degrees were in education, and their first jobs in New Hampshire were in that field. Anna's family lived in the Lake Winnipesauke school district. Within weeks of their arrival, they both had jobs. They worked those jobs until the summer of Lucy's fifth birthday. It was after the mess from the birthday party had been cleaned up, and Lucy was asleep in her bed, that Anna declared they had saved enough money for the down payment on the house she wanted. Eli looked across their rented front porch at her beautiful face as it lit up with flashes of heat lightning and grinned his unqualified assent. She determined they would buy the old Hampton Place and do all the renovations and modernizing themselves. Eventually, and she knew this as plainly as she knew her own name, it would grow into the best bed-and-breakfast on the East Coast. Two years later, when her idea was beginning to pay dividends for both of them, she was gone.

In the four years since, Eli vacillated between wanting to sell the place at half its value to get as far away from it as possible and wanting it to be so successful he could open a whole chain throughout all of New England. He settled on the in-between place of running the most highly-rated bed-and-breakfast, according to TripAdvisor, in the state of New Hampshire. As an homage to the woman he loved the way a child loves Christmas, he renamed the bed-and-breakfast after her with the simplest form of memorial he could imagine. It was now known as Anna's Place.

Thinking of Christmas caused another bout of anxiety in Eli. In this case, that anxiety was justified. There were only four days, including today, to get everything ready. Now that Vincent had invited these podcasters from Los Angeles to come experience Christmas in Dayton, Eli felt he was under a larger microscope than was typical. People came to Dayton from all the surrounding counties in New Hampshire to see the Christmas display put on by the town. Most years, they were able to build a North Pole-like village out on the ice. The exceptional cold the town experienced so far this winter meant Santa's Village was a fully functioning tourist attraction by this late date.

Since Christmas had been Anna's favorite time of the year, Eli embraced the holiday even more than when she was alive. He did it all for Lucy, of course, but he had made such a big production of it at the bed-and-breakfast these last four years that Vincent put him in charge of Christmas for the whole town this season. The main duty lay in supervising the construction of the village, but that duty, in addition to running the bed-and-breakfast, was more than enough to stress him out. Fortunately for him, most people preferred to spend Christmas with their loved ones. So, other than the LA podcasters, he only had one other couple booked for Christmas.

Vincent had asked Eli to be the Santa Village project manager while the two men were sitting at the Thanksgiving dinner table enjoying the early stages of tryptophan comas. The very same deep feelings of sleepiness scientists now said weren't real. Vincent groggily reminded Eli, Anna would have loved to see him take on this responsibility for the town. Naturally, that was the precise moment Lucy chose to come in from the Turner family living room. Vincent completed his pitch while Lucy sat down beside her father. She heard enough to ask what was going on. At that point, what choice did Eli have? He accepted against his better judgment.

Now, he only had three days left to round out a magnificent Christmas Eve on the Ice celebration, or risk disappointing his daughter's memory of her mother. In other words, she might hit him with one of those 'if he really loved my mom, he should have done a much better job than this' kind of things. To see Lucy disappointed at Christmastime would be more than Eli could bear. No matter what difficulties they had during the rest of the year, Eli always made sure Christmas was seamless. He certainly didn't intend to ruin his perfect track record this year. The podcasters from Los Angeles, combined with the extra duties as custodian of the Christmas Spirit for all of Dayton, were threatening to overturn the balance Eli worked so hard to maintain in his and Lucy's life.

Speaking of the podcasters from Los Angeles, where in the heck were they? It was now a quarter after one. Eli had called Ian as a precaution. He hadn't intended to need his help. These big-city podcasters were going to cause him to miss being there, for the first time in either of their lives, when his daughter stepped off the school bus. That was not acceptable. Eli picked up his phone. Scrolled through the contacts until he found Vincent's number. He was about to complete the call when he saw a twin-engine Cessna touching down on the runway. He glanced at his watch. It was only 1:17. If the podcasters were in his SUV by 1:30, they would make it home in plenty of time. If they weren't in his SUV by 1:30, Vincent would be reimbursing them for a mighty expensive cab fare. He closed the contact on his phone... for now.

Eli thought he could speed things up a bit if he pulled his SUV into the first available slot in the parking lot next to the tiny airport's exit. Determined to accomplish this before they disembarked, he hurried out to the parking lot and executed the time-saving maneuver. He was opening the rear of the SUV when a friendly hand tapped him on the shoulder.

"Is there any chance you're Eli Ryder?" The new

voice asked.

Eli turned to face two well-dressed women wrangling a half dozen wheeled suitcases between them. Eli was stunned. His heart forgot how to beat properly for far longer than could possibly be healthy. When it remembered, or at least submitted to the fact that beating was its job, it did so with a mildly paralytic jolt. He would not have disputed a doctor who told him his internal temperature had lowered by four or five degrees. "Tha..." His voice came out scratchy. Nothing like what he usually sounded like. He tried again. "That's me." Much better. Still, if either of those women had an ounce of perception available to them, they both knew Eli thought Paige possessed world-stopping beauty.

"My name is Paige Langford." Paige extended her hand, and Eli took it in his. There was no way he could know it, but the palpitations going on in his body in that moment were duplicating themselves in her. She thought this vision of rustic manliness standing in front of her also possessed world-stopping handsomeness. She barely remembered to introduce her co-host and fellow traveler. "This is Jessica Keller."

As soon as Paige and Eli quit shaking hands, Jessica offered hers. "Is it always this cold here, Eli? The temperature was close to 80 when we left Los Angeles eight hours ago. I suppose with the time change, it's more like eleven hours ago. Whatever about the time, I didn't mean to get distracted talking about that. It was the temperature difference I really wanted to go on about. I am an extremely cold-blooded girl."

Eli smiled over Jessica's soliloquy to warmer temperatures. Paige thought the smile made him look even more handsome. "Believe it or not, this is kind of a warm spell for us." He moved to the side to offer up the rear area of his vehicle for the suitcases. "Please, put your things in here." He cast a sideways glance at the number of suitcases Paige and Jessica shepherded. "You may have to put some in the backseat." He took another glance at the number of suitcases. "You may even have to put some on the floorboards."

Paige could tell Eli was worried the large cargo capacity of his SUV was not going to be sufficient to accommodate the full spectrum of clothing options Paige and Jessica had brought with them. She interceded on behalf of his anxiety. "If we can't fit everything in right now, we can always leave some bags here and come back and pick them up after we rent a car in Dayton."

Paige's words reassured Eli they wouldn't waste unnecessary time trying to redesign the space inside his vehicle if the suitcases didn't fit naturally. "Perfect!"

He helped the women load their belongings. They were able to fit all the suitcases into the SUV with very little of that space-redesigning he thought they were in for when they were standing on the sidewalk. The last suitcase would have to coexist in some capacity with Jessica's long legs, but nothing had to be left at the airport.

After spending more time than Eli thought was required studying the spatial constraints of the rear cabin area, Jessica determined she would rather rest her feet on the suitcase than straddle it all the way to Dayton. With everything finally loaded, Eli circled around to the passenger side to let his passengers in while he held the door for them. He looked at his watch as he closed the door. It was 1:32. In spite of all that happened, he was only two minutes behind his ultimatum time. Everything was going to be fine. He wouldn't be late to pick Lucy up. She wouldn't have to wonder where her father was when she stepped off that bus. Of course, that didn't mean he would call and cancel Ian coming out to the house as an insurance policy. No parent ever knew when something unforeseen could happen to derail a perfectly formulated plan. Since he was still so far away, and there was still so little room for error, he decided against letting Ian off the hook. However, barring a flat tire, or some other failure in the SUV's ability to move forward at sixty miles per hour, there was no way he was going to be late.

His anxiety over Lucy subsided as he walked around the front of the SUV. It allowed space in his brain for him to wonder what that thing was that had happened to him when he first saw Paige. The only time he had ever remembered feeling that way before was all the way back in his first semester in college. To be precise, it was the day he first met Anna at the Curry School library. They had both gone there to study because their roommates were being too loud. The fact that he hadn't gotten much studying done that night once he met her hadn't mattered to him at the time. After she left, he'd stayed in the library until the sun came up, trying to memorize the material for his exam. He hadn't minded that either. What was lack of sleep when compared with meeting a once-in-a-lifetime individual?

She had been worth it that first sleepless night. She had been worth it every additional night he had been fortunate enough to share with her in the years that piled up between then and her passing. Anna had been the only time someone captured his attention from the first moment he met them. Or, Anna had been the only time *until* he met Paige. What in the world did that mean? And how would he explain it to any of the people who shared his life with him in Dayton?

Eli shook his head slightly to clear it of the illusion. It was nothing. It meant nothing. Paige was a beautiful woman. His nervous system had been impressed by this fact. That was all. His reaction to her was a simple matter of biology and pheromones. As he grasped the door handle of his SUV, Eli felt this ultra-brief pep talk with himself had given him more control over his emotions. For a moment, it almost seemed as if he were coming close to betraying Anna's memory. Now that he could write it off as a physical reaction to Paige's beauty, he felt better. It wasn't love at first sight. That idea was ridiculous. It was, like he said, the science of pheromones… and facial symmetries, maybe. Right? If that were right, why did he lack all confidence in a positive answer? Also, why did it feel to him like he really was betraying Anna?

As he settled into his seat and started the SUV, he wondered what his daughter would think of the palpitations in his heart if she knew of them. Eli spent the last four years religiously focused on making two things true for his daughter. The first was that she was as properly adjusted to the loss of her mother as any reasonable person could expect her to be. The second was that she knew her father tried, every day, to honor his memory of her mother by making the business she started flourish.

The idea that there might be someone else in the world for him never entered his mind. In other words, he hadn't even thought about looking for a date, much less going out on one. He was defined by his fatherhood and his business. Paige was a distraction of physiology, which would quickly fade. She wouldn't live up to her first impression. How often did that happen? People were never as great as you thought they were when you first met them. Especially when that first impression of them was that they were one of the most beautiful people on the planet. Eli laughed to himself as he pulled out onto the road that would take him back to Dayton. She had set the bar so high, there was no way she could clear it again.

He had no idea how wrong he was.

CHAPTER THREE

As Eli predicted, he pulled in at the bus stop fifteen minutes before the bus was due to arrive. This was ten minutes later than he usually got there, but only he and the trees would ever know that fact. Ian waited serenely in his pickup with just the smallest of smiles on his face to suggest he knew all along his presence wasn't going to be necessary. Eli pulled in beside him and rolled the window down on his SUV. "Thank you, sir."

"No problem. At this point in our friendship, I don't feel like I have to say it out loud but, just in case I do, you know I'd be anywhere, at any time, for you or Lucy." Ian surveyed the inside of Eli's SUV. "These must be our famous influencers from the internet. The ones who've come to Dayton to be infected by our Christmas spirit."

Jessica spoke up first. Paige imagined that whatever that thing was that happened between her and Eli when they first met, was happening to Jessica right now, with Ian. Jessica was smitten by the aura of this New England cowboy and his jacked-up truck. "For the record, only one of us needs infecting. I'm Jessica Keller, and I'm a true believer." Jessica picked out Paige in the front seat with her eyes. "The Scrooge is in the front seat."

Paige laughed. "The Scrooge disagrees with the characterization but admits that others might see it that way. My real name is Paige Langford, by the way."

Ian acknowledged the introductions with a nod of his head. "Pleased to meet both of you."

Eli had one more favor to ask of Ian. "Would you mind running these two up to the house in my car so they can unload their luggage?"

"Not at all." Ian opened the door of his truck as Eli did the same with his SUV. Right before they switched vehicles, Eli clapped Ian on the shoulder like a brother. It was a small expression of gratitude, but one Eli felt was necessary. He knew words were not sufficient to thank Ian for dropping everything he was doing in the middle of his day to come and be there for Lucy, on the off chance she needed him. Eli hoped the shoulder clap conveyed his appreciation more deeply than the verbal 'thank you' he gave when they first pulled up beside Ian's truck.

Eli addressed Paige and Jessica. "My daughter's bus should be here in the next ten minutes. If you two don't want to wait for me to show you around up at the house, you can unload all your stuff into either of the rooms on the left-hand side of the upstairs hall."

"Take your time. We're in no hurry." Paige spoke for both her and Jessica because she knew Jessica wouldn't mind. After waiting for her to finish speaking, Ian dropped Eli's SUV into drive and idled up the driveway toward the bed-and-breakfast.

A few minutes later, Eli heard the bus coming before he could see it. He got out of Ian's truck and walked toward the edge of the road. He stood there in the cold New Hampshire air thinking how much Lucy reminded him of Anna. She had always looked just like her mom, but in the last couple of years she had developed that ebullience of personality that had been Anna's most magnetic feature. To know Anna was to love her. She was like a neutron star. Once you fell into her orbit, there was no escaping her pull. Eli could tell it was going to be the same way with Lucy.

That ebullience was characterized by a way of being so excited about even the most mundane of activities, anyone in her presence caught the excitement too, like a virus only without the negative connotation. It was a fascinating thing to watch. Eli knew, if he lived to be a hundred, he would never tire of bearing witness to the phenomenon. And that's exactly what his daughter was to him—a phenomenon. It was the explanation for why he engaged in the habit of helicopter parenting. Lucy was a force of nature. An act of God. Eli wouldn't bother about whatever words you chose to describe her as long as you captured the main idea. Lucy was special. The same way Anna had been special. Eli's mission on this planet was to be sure he didn't fail a second time in protecting the special thing he had been given to protect.

All these thoughts helped him to understand himself. He admitted Paige may have thrown him into a momentary hiccup of doubt with her excessive attractiveness. However, he knew who he was essentially. He was a caretaker of the world's most precious gift, an exceptional child. Eli felt all the presses could stop in that moment because there it was, perfectly lucid comprehension. His primary role as caretaker explained why he had never cared to 'date' someone after Anna passed. He didn't want to disappoint the world by being distracted from the seriousness of the job which fell onto his broad shoulders. What difference did loneliness make in the face of the responsibility the universe gave him? Was he lonely? As hard as it was for him to believe it, he hadn't wrestled with that idea before this very moment.

It was the last thought he had in that vein before the bus pulled up and opened its doors. It released that precious gift, the one that caused this long series of mind digressions, back into his immediate care. Lucy ran across the space which separated him from her and threw her bookbag at him as she approached. He caught it. The way he did every day. He then pretended to fall backward from its weight. The way he did every day. "My favorite daughter returns!"

Lucy shook her head at her father. Anyone watching would by now have caught on that they had been doing this same routine every time she got off the bus, for the last four years. "Dad, I'm your only daughter." She said it with a tone that mimicked mild exasperation but was really one hundred percent joy.

Eli put on a mask of shock. "Are you serious?"

"As a heart attack." Lucy pointed at Ian's jacked-up truck. "Why are you driving Uncle Ian's truck?" Lucy couldn't spend as much time with her overly-anxious helicoptering father as she did, and not become adept at noticing anything out of the ordinary.

"I asked him to come by just in case I was late getting back from the airport." Eli said as he followed his daughter back toward Ian's truck.

"Did you get them?" Lucy seemed especially interested in the answer to this.

"Yeah. They were running late. That's why I called

Ian, but I got them. They're up in the house now." Eli opened the passenger door for his daughter. She climbed up into the front seat. He began to shut it when his daughter interrupted the motion with a question.

"Is she nice, Dad?" Lucy hadn't wanted to ask, but her body wouldn't mind her will. She knew the look in her eyes was going to be a dead giveaway, so she directed her gaze out the front window when she said it. Then she felt that was even more of a dead giveaway since she never talked like that. She just wasn't going to be able to hide it. She cared about the answer to this question much more than she had a right to care about it. Her dad was going to see right through her.

Eli knew something was up with his daughter. Her inability to find a subject for her eyes to rest on made that clear, but he was clueless as to what it might be. Of course, her immediate question had to be referring to the podcasters. He wasn't sure which one she was talking about. He didn't want to guess Paige because that might tip his hand that Paige had impacted him more than normal, so he went with a generic, "They're both nice." Eli could tell she accepted that answer for now, so he shut the door and walked around to the driver's side of the truck.

All the way from the bottom of his driveway to the top, he listened to his daughter tell him about her day. Despite his attempt to give his daughter his full attention, a part of him wondered why she wanted to know if 'she' was 'nice'. He had told her the day before that a couple of podcasters would be staying with them through Christmas. At the time, he had been surprised by the fact she hadn't asked him for the definition of podcaster. It never occurred to him that she might be looking forward to seeing them. And that's what this reaction from Lucy looked like to him, anticipation. She was eager to meet one of the podcasters. All that remained was to determine which one, and why. He would pay close attention to her initial reactions to Paige and Jessica to see if he could figure it out without having to ask.

When they got to the house, Lucy had her seat belt off and her door open before Eli got Ian's truck completely parked. She flew toward the front door with her bookbag flopping from one shoulder the way kids wore them these days. The depth of her reaction combined with its eleven-year-old lack of subtlety convinced Eli there, absolutely, was something going on with his daughter. That something had to do with the podcasters who had invaded his bed-and-breakfast. It was now his mission to figure out why.

He had been listening to the podcasts for the last few days. That was true. He thought he had done it inconspicuously, and on his own time. After Vincent asked him if he had room to let the podcasters stay in his bed-and-breakfast for the last few days leading up to Christmas, and he admitted he did, he felt it was his due diligence to have some idea what they were like. It was also true that Lucy had occasionally been in the common room doing her homework while he listened. Could she have been listening too? Had something Paige said resonated with Lucy in a way that would make her act the way she had been acting since the bus stop?

Good Lord, he hoped it wasn't that anti-Christmas message Paige recorded. The thing that had been the impetus for this whole bet between her and Vincent. How would he ever reconcile anti-Christmas sentiment with Lucy being Anna's daughter? Perhaps he had made a gigantic mistake when he allowed Vincent to book the podcasters at Anna's Place. Look at all the lights, wreaths, and other Christmas decorations just on the front porch of his bed-and-breakfast. How could Lucy come home from school every day to this outpost of intense Christmas spirit and not feel the love for the holiday her mother felt? It was impossible to believe. Eli was almost angry with himself for thinking such horrible thoughts. It had to be something else.

As he laid his hand on the knob of his front door, Eli's internal monitoring system was flashing a warning to him. He needed to calm down. His anxiety had risen by three or more octaves since Paige had tapped him on the shoulder. If anxiety were a singing voice, he thought, his would have gone from a baritone to a soprano over the last few hours. This idea Lucy might have been impressed by Paige's argument against the Christmas spirit had put down deep roots in his brain. He was growing surer by the moment this hypothesis was correct.

If true, it was obviously all his fault. Had he bothered to explain why he was listening, instead of assuming it wouldn't catch her interest, and therefore didn't matter, he wouldn't be in this position right now. Lucy had always been a diehard Christmas enthusiast. He never imagined it was possible she could be anything else. He shook his head and grimaced at his own failure to think things through. He opened the door to his house, determined to find out what was going on with his Lucy.

He could hear his daughter's voice, and the excitement that infused it, coming from the common room. She sounded like someone meeting her primary idol for the first time. She sounded like a... fan. Eli felt unprepared. Somehow, he had missed everything. It was unlike him to be unaware when it came to his daughter. The feeling was so alien to his parental DNA; he didn't know what to do. He thought he had himself trained to notice everything that went on in her world. How had he missed her obvious fascination with Paige? When had she found the time to develop this fascination? Had it been during the few hours he spent listening to Paige's show in her presence? It couldn't have been much more than six hours, seven at the most.

His preoccupation with what he perceived as his fatherly shortcomings was so intense, he considered slowing his pace so he could hear a few sentences of what Lucy, Paige, and Jessica were saying before entering the common room. He decided against the tactic, but only because it was too weird. Even for the current, caterwauling state of his anxiety, it was too weird. Instead, he closed his eyes and counted to five to calm his nerves. He then entered the room, doing his best impression of normal.

Lucy was in the middle of a substantial oration when he entered. She stood directly in front of Paige. All her attention was focused on Paige in a way that made it obvious to the grownups in the room she thought Paige was 'super cool'. Ian and Jessica watched the display with smiles that showed they thought Lucy was being 'super cute'. Despite his attempts at normal, Eli looked confused.

"I want to be a writer when I get older, like you." These words from Lucy didn't help Eli sort his mental state. The last time he talked with Lucy about what she wanted to be, she was positive she would be a veterinarian. Admittedly, they hadn't had the conversation within the last few days, but it couldn't have been more than six months ago either.

"Have you written anything yet?" Paige wanted to know.

"Just a couple of things," Lucy began. "I have one short story I'm kind of proud of. Mrs. Atwell, my homeroom teacher, said it was good."

Eli imagined the bricks were destined to keep falling on his head all afternoon. Who was this person standing in the common room of his bed-and-breakfast, and what had she done with his daughter? This was the first Eli had ever heard about a short story Lucy was 'kind of proud of'. As the strain of all these new and foreign thoughts tightened their cords around his anxiety, Eli suddenly realized Mrs. Atwell was the real source of his information problem.

How had she not mentioned she thought his daughter was a budding novelist? In the same way he had never been late to the bus stop in Lucy's life, he had also never skipped a parent-teacher conference. Yet, this novelist ambition of Lucy's had never come up before this very minute. The next parent-teacher conference was liable to be livelier than usual. That was, if he didn't call Mrs. Atwell tonight. She was, after all, Anna's connection in the Dayton school district, and Lucy's great-aunt to boot. Eli inhaled deeply to settle himself. He knew he was getting too wound up about this infatuation Lucy had with Paige. He told himself to calm down before he said something silly. Something he might regret later.

"Any chance I could read it?" Paige asked.

Eli watched as Lucy dissolved into an oasis of delight. It looked to him as though Paige had made her whole Christmas. "Oh, I couldn't ask you to do that." Eli shook his head. Lucy might have only been eleven, but she was acting like a miniature adult. When had she learned it was proper to give a person an out in case they accidentally offered to do something they didn't really want to do?

"I would be honored." Paige loved that Lucy deflected her initial offer to read her story. It was a clear sign of a future author.

"In that case, yes," Lucy replied. "I'd like to do some revising on it first, though. If that's okay?"

"Of course," Paige agreed. "I'll give you my email address too. In case you don't have it ready before I leave. I don't want to put you under pressure to hand over work you feel isn't finished. That's something you can wait to experience until later on in your life as a writer." Paige and Lucy shared a conspiratorial laugh together. The sort of thing people in the same profession do when they bond over a commonality. They were like two retail workers talking about grumpy customers during the holiday season. Eli had heard enough, or hadn't heard enough, depending on which way he looked at it. He resolved to let his presence be recognized within the room. "Well, I see you two have met my daughter."

Paige immediately spoke up. "Yes, and she wants to be a writer, which is fascinating." Lucy's face bloomed with delight when Paige listed her future occupation as writer.

Eli looked at Lucy while an impish grin spread

across his face. "I find it pretty fascinating too, since she never mentioned it to me."

Lucy immediately felt bad. She dropped her eyes to the floor. In all her life, she had never kept anything from her father. Of course, she knew why she had picked her aunt's reaction to her silly story as the place to start. She didn't have the heart to show it to him because the story was about how much the main character missed having a mom. She didn't want her Dad thinking the things Lucy wrote about in her story were somehow his fault. Like, if he had been a better Dad, Lucy wouldn't have written a story in which the main character felt sad about not having a mom. That wasn't the point of her story at all. But she was afraid that was the way her Dad would see it. For that reason, and only that reason, she kept the story a secret from him, a fact which now left her feeling terrible. "Sorry, Dad. I kept meaning to tell you, but something else always came up." Lucy heard how lame that excuse sounded, but it was the best she could come up with on the spur of the moment. Why had she been so comfortable with Paige? Barely two minutes after meeting her, and she had brought her story up. She knew her timing was horrible. She should have waited for the chance to talk to Paige when no one else was around.

Eli gathered there was more to the case of the Mrs. Atwell approved short story than Lucy was letting on, but he wasn't the type of dad to press the issue. He had seen her face go from joyous to embarrassed in less than two seconds. He knew he was the culprit. She would tell him about her desire to be a writer when she was good and ready. Notwithstanding the fact that his supreme goal in life was to be the world's most excellent father, he still couldn't completely let Lucy off the hook without seizing the chance to build on a teachable moment. "Well, as the great Virginia Woolf once said: If you do not tell the truth about yourself..."

Paige interrupted him, in numb struck automaton tones, to finish the quote, "You cannot tell it about other people." She then looked at him as though he were something other than a male of the human species... a giant salamander, maybe. After her numbness subsided slightly, she was able to eke out, "That is, literally, my favorite quote, by my favorite author." Paige shook her head in disbelief that Eli knew that particular passage. "It is also, in my humble opinion, one of the truest things ever said on the subject of writing."

A semi-awkward silence descended on the common room as Paige and Eli studied each other to try and work out what was going on with their physiologies. Was this thing developing between them real or in their heads? Thankfully for Eli, who was suffering through another of those heart palpitations and couldn't find his words, Ian came to his rescue. "Eli, did you want to show the ladies their rooms, or should I?"

Lucy piped up. "Oh, Dad, let me. Let me. Please?"

Once again, what choice did Eli have? "Of course you can, Lucy."

CHAPTER FOUR

The world has raised its whip; where will it descend.

Paige remembered this quote from Mrs. Dalloway as she went through the motions of occupying her body with the small task of setting up her room to pass the time. Paige used the aphorism whenever she felt like saying what other people said when they went with 'the die is cast'. She did not want to be all alone in her room reciting Virginia Woolf quotes to herself. She would prefer going over to Jessica's room to see if their initial impressions of the small town of Dayton correlated, but Jessica had accepted a ride into said small town of Dayton from Ian, in order to rent a car for their stay. Left to her own devices, and with the trifling amount of work that needed to be done to set up her room completed within ten minutes, Paige found herself sitting at the big picture window gazing out onto Lake Winnipesaukee.

Now that all the introductions were out of the way and she had a minute to appreciate things in her own mind without the distraction of having to make conversation, she admitted this place was stunningly beautiful. Her room was tastefully elegant with its light hardwood floors, built-in fireplace, enormous king-sized bed with what looked like a solid oak headboard, and a view which seemed more painting than real. Of course, the Christmas decorations were wildly over the top, but she wasn't ready to pick any fights over that just yet. Besides, there were a lot of decorations in her room, including her very own tree, but the decorations were tasteful as well as numerous. If forced, she might even grant she kind of liked them. Something about the red and green accents matched the frosty world outside and complemented the deep wooden earthy tones inside her room. It all came together to produce a soothing effect.

Paige stacked up the pillows on her big wooden bed until they resembled something in the neighborhood of a chair. She wiggled her way into this ode to relaxation she had made and focused her attention out the window and onto the beauty of the lake. As she tried to coerce her doubts about this trip into leaving her mind, she wondered if she would have more success if she weren't sitting on top of a Christmas comforter.

Now that she was here and had met Eli and his adorable daughter, Lucy, she was infinitely more positive than when she'd been back in Los Angeles that coming here was an atrocious mistake. Eli and Lucy were wonderful people. Their little town of Dayton looked, to Paige's jaded big-city eyes, like a small-town Christmas Utopia. She could not perpetrate the dishonesty she, Jessica, and Mr. Turner cooked up on these beautiful people. Her thoughts of people not knowing they were deceived reminded her again of Virginia Woolf's words. The same ones that had recently left Eli's lips. How in the world had he managed to come up with Paige's absolute, all time, favorite quote from her absolute all-time favorite author? It was creepy. She imagined that there weren't more than a handful of people on the planet who knew that quote by heart. How was it that he knew it and used it on the very day he met her… the world's biggest Virginia Woolf fan?

Most people would take the coincidence as a sign of good things to come. Paige took it as an indication her intentions in Dayton were doomed from the start. She thought about putting the tab for this trip on her MasterCard. That would eliminate the guilt she felt. Then, she could use the next episode in her podcast to tell the world the truth about why she accepted Mr. Turner's modest proposal. The revelation would ruin the show by destroying the faith her audience had in her, but at least she would stop feeling like an imposter in her own skin.

People would forgive her too. Eventually. She was certain of that because she wasn't doing any of this for personal gain. She was doing it for Jessica. That last thought hung in the Christmassy air of her room. It did not sit well among the shelves filled with holly and eight tiny reindeer. It reminded her of another quote. This one was from Eliot and his Murder in the Cathedral. It was about how doing the right thing, for the wrong reason, was the greatest treason. Paige squinted her eyes and gritted her teeth. Lord, sometimes she really did hate being an English major. This would be so much easier for her if she had majored in math. The ethical calculus in any practical situation always favored helping a friend over telling the truth. Why was she holding herself hostage to the overly complicated ethics instilled in her by her humanities professors?

It wasn't long before her mind vacated the section of itself where it held her responsible for every bad thing that happened in her world and returned to thinking of

Eli. Her attraction to him had been instantaneous and direct. She didn't remember ever feeling that way about another person before. Was this the feeling people talked about when they claimed to have fallen in love... At First Sight? Paige reminded herself that no one over the age of eleven believed fairy-tale ideas like love at first sight existed in the real world. She thought there was more chance she would embrace Christmas, and all its commodified glory, than allow herself to believe in the silliness known as love at first sight.

Although she allowed the idea was an interesting object for study. It might pass for something her author's nature enshrined in a book one day. She could see herself aligning two of her characters so perfectly with each other and the universe, they fell instantly in love. However, she was not prepared to admit anything in the real world could appear, fully formed, from the luminiferous ether, and bear any serious resemblance to the most beautiful idea humans had ever invented. Love was built from the accumulation of tiny gestures of selflessness that got caught in the net of hundreds of days.

Paige insisted to herself that there was no chance her follow-up thought, which circled through her mind at high speed, was ever going to happen. She entertained it merely for the sake of completing an argument which was philosophically interesting to her. With that proviso officially noted, she pondered the idea that, even if she and Eli were to fall in love one day, far in the future, it would not mean that what she was feeling right now was accurately characterized by the expression, love at first sight. It would just be a coincidence of timing and biology.

Paige lightly thumped the side of her head with her hand. It was a physical cue to her brain to quit short-circuiting over Eli and her ridiculous attraction to him. He had a daughter. His house was more than three thousand miles from her house. He probably didn't feel the same way about Paige that she felt about him. All those things were good points, and she acknowledged them with as much of her rationality as she could muster. And yet, there he was. Occupying her mind again. She feared she would go on spending too much of her time thinking about him until she knew for certain one way or the other. Did he also feel something for her?

Since the thumping trick was obviously failing to provide her any relief, Paige tried to clear her head by shaking it fiercely. She then looked around the room to find something to distract herself. At last she found it. Beside the reproduction of Monet's 'Waterloo Bridge' on the far wall, a solitary shelf housed a few books. Paige leapt out of bed with renewed purpose. She was a radical advocate for the idea that you could learn anything you wanted to know about a person by quickly browsing through the books they chose to keep around them. The task grew tougher in recent years with the advent of digital books, but, she reasoned, that made the books people did choose to keep around them, in physical form, that much more special.

She decided the shelf was primarily intended as decoration. The degree of difficulty in learning anything meaningful from a decorative bookshelf was astronomical. Fortunately, Paige was a virtuoso at character deduction by book titles owned. Before letting the words on the spines sink into her brain, she first poured her attention into evaluating the area surrounding the books for clues. The shelf they rested on was battered and bruised, like it had been moved several times before being installed in its current resting place. There were small chips in the woodwork, which revealed the untreated wood beneath the varnish. Paige felt confident the shelf had been loved as much for its function as for its form. True lovers of books were the only types of people who put that much effort into the things that housed them. Her attachment to Eli was not lessening, like she had hoped it might, by completing this activity.

There were only five books on the shelf, which meant Paige was able to catch all the titles in a single glance from left to right. The first three were typical fare along the modern genre categories. They were the obligatory bookshelf stalwarts of mystery, legal, and romance. They were written by authors who were equally as obligatory as the genres they wrote in. If for no other reason than that they had become so famous. The fourth was wildly interesting to her. It was one of her favorite books from the 1950s. Ralph Ellison's only novel published during his lifetime. Mr. Ellison's story forced her into a reevaluation of most all of her values when she read it the first time some fifteen years ago. What more could you ask from a book than that?

The title of the fifth book sounded in her brain like a long crack of thunder boiling up from a darkening horizon. She dared not look at it too long. Obviously, that comment about Virginia Woolf, which had left Eli's lips no more than twenty minutes ago, had not been an accident. The last book on the shelf was Mrs. Dalloway.

Paige took the Ellison book down because she could not bear to take the Woolf book down. She absent-mindedly thumbed through it as she thought about other things. What did all this mean? Was it possible the universe was trying to tell her something? At what point did the flow of coincidence coalesce into intention? More importantly, how could Paige judge that scenario accurately when she was the one under the spell of the coincidences?

And there it was, in black and white, in her own mind. She had said it herself, 'under the spell of'. The only things you could be 'under the spell of' were imaginary things. It made her feel better to have reasoned her way to the end of her dilemma. Now that she saw she was under a spell; she could begin the process of dissociating from whatever emotions she was having. She wasn't in love with Eli. That was silly. She had fallen, temporarily, under his spell. That was all.

She replaced the Ellison book. She was confident she had put to rest any foolish notions she might have been developing. She permitted herself a smile at the porcelain Santa, which acted as a bookend. The way he had his hands out pushing against the books was too cute to ignore. She wondered who had been responsible for that little piece of humor. Was it Eli? Lucy? Or, had someone else's hands contributed to the design choices in this room? Paige was ready to sit at the desk in her room and go through some more of the emails from the fans of her show when someone knocked on her door. "Who is it?" Paige asked as she walked toward the sound.

"It's me." Lucy raised her voice so Paige would be

able to hear her.

Paige opened the door. "Well, come on in." She stepped to the side to allow Lucy into the room with her.

Lucy smiled politely and walked into Paige's room. "Dad wanted me to ask you if you'd like a tour of the house and all the things we have to offer before it gets too dark outside to see. Normally, he gives that tour, but I asked him if I could do it this time. Just like I asked if I could show you and Jessica up to your rooms. If you don't want to, or if you want him to do it, I'll understand." Lucy hung her head. The request was already defeated in her mind. She was waiting around for Paige to make it official. On what planet would a successful thirty-five-year-old woman choose to hang out with an eleven-year-old kid?

"I'd love that, actually. Let me grab my coat." Paige retrieved her coat from the chair in front of the desk that contained her laptop.

"Oh, wow, that's awesome." Lucy was too young to be any good at hiding her surprise. She was still on the what you see is what you get rung of human development.

Paige met up with Lucy in the center of her room. Her coat draped over her arm. "Outside tour first, or inside tour first?" she asked.

"I thought we'd start with the inside." Lucy studied the floor. She was having a hard time stating her preferences to Paige. "If that's okay with you." Obviously, she didn't want to jeopardize Paige's desire to spend time with her by suggesting something Paige didn't want to do.

Paige had been in Lucy's shoes a couple of times before. The first time she remembered it happening was with one of her high school teachers. Paige would never forget the day Mrs. Burratti read her personal essay out loud in front of the class as an example of what good writing sounded like. Of course, it happened again with a couple of Paige's college professors, who also advocated she put in the necessary time to develop her writing skills. Paige recognized she was a bit of a hero, in that Mrs. Burratti-type way, to Lucy, because she had been through these same dramas in her own life. If Paige played her cards correctly, and Lucy continued on this path she had chosen, there was a strong chance Paige would be thanked in the acknowledgements section of one of Lucy's future books. Lucy would call her out for being one of the first adults, outside her family, to encourage her writing impulse. Paige knew this was true from experience. The acknowledgment section of her first novel contained a brief thank you to none other than, Mrs. Burratti.

Paige could tell Lucy struggled with the idea that she really wanted to spend time with her. This impression of Lucy's wasn't going to go away easily. Paige would have to keep restating her desire until Lucy developed confidence in it. "Inside works for me." Paige said as she gave Lucy a small pat on the shoulder in the hopes the gesture would steady Lucy's nerves.

Lucy led Paige into the hallway while simultaneously reciting the history of her father's bed-and-breakfast. Her delivery was perfect, so Paige knew she must have heard Eli deliver these same words dozens of times before. "The upstairs portion of the main house has three bedrooms which are available to the general public." Lucy walked toward the open door on the right side of the hall. "You and your friend Jessica have the bedrooms with the lakeside view." She leaned in conspiratorially toward Paige. "Lucky you," she said in a half-whisper.

Lucy paused the recital to go further off script for a moment. "Dad made sure you and Jessica got those even though they rent out for twice what the other bedroom up here goes for." It seemed Lucy wanted Paige to know that her father had sacrificed something by letting her stay there. Lucy realized that didn't quite explain how it was any sort of sacrifice, so she added the missing element even though it was chronologically out of place. "Mr. Turner asked if Dad would take a discounted rate for your rooms because he thinks it will eventually be so good for tourism." Now Lucy wondered if she had gone too far in the other direction. It would be the worst if Paige thought she were a burden on her father's business. "Not that he minded holding the rooms for you. And we don't generally book up this close to Christmas anyway." Lucy stopped in the doorway of the room with no lakeside view. She looked like she was about three more off-script sentences away from breaking down into tears. "I feel like I'm making everything sound horrible," she lamented.

Paige laughed out loud despite her better judgment. "Oh, Lucy, sweetheart. You are precious and wonderful, and I am very happy you and your father have allowed Jessica and I to stay in your beautiful home."

Lucy exhaled with relief. "Thank you, Paige. I don't know what's come over me. I've done this speech twenty times if I've done it once. I never mess it up." Lucy shook her head at the way she had let her excitement over meeting Paige overturn her skill at conducting the tour.

"Well, I think you are doing an incredible job, and I think you should act like you were going into your next point and forget about the mistakes you think you made." Paige then gave Lucy a small hug as a gesture of support. It happened naturally, with no forethought. Not surprisingly, it made them both feel better.

Lucy took Paige's advice by jumping right back into the tour as though she had never deserted her script. "Usually, each room has a separate theme." Lucy pointed at the abundance of Christmas decorations in the room. "Starting on December 1st, Dad and I redo all the rooms in the accoutrements of the holiday spirit." Lucy halted her monologue again to give Paige a language lover's smile. "I stole that word from Dad. He's always using big words like that. He says he can't help it because he majored in English, but I think he just likes throwing big words around."

"A man after my own heart." She wasn't saying it just to be saying it either. The ability to explain the way she loved words was impossible unless the person she was explaining it to also had some form of the same weakness. Like anyone else, she could be inspired by a wonderful painting or a heartfelt piece of music. However, neither of those experiences, no matter how great the artist or composer, compared to the first time she had read The Brothers Karamazov, or the first time she read Hughes' poem Harlem. For her, a connoisseur of words, letter combinations were just different than all other forms of art.

Lucy was happy to hear Paige claim her father as one of her own. For a reason which was not clear to her conscious mind, she chose to egg on Paige's response. "My Dad loves to read, by the way." Lucy walked toward the stairs. She was continuing the tour while adding to Paige's conception of her father. "We go to the bookstore every week. He buys me one new book each time. Right now, I'm reading A Wrinkle in Time." Lucy looked up at Paige for confirmation.

"You've read that one, haven't you?"

"It's one of my favorites." Paige answered truthfully.

"I knew you would have read it." Lucy stopped at the bottom of the stairs. "Do you think you could give me a book to read? I mean, not the actual book, of course, just a title. And then when Dad and I go to the bookstore after Christmas, I can choose the one you suggest."

"No problem. It'll be a trade." Paige looked at Lucy with a mild bit of mischief in her expression. "I'll give you a book, but only after you let me read your story."

Lucy's face brightened. She had resolved not to mention her story again because it had felt like she had imposed on Paige when she had asked her to read it earlier. The fact Paige brought it back up on her own was proof enough to Lucy that Paige actually wanted to read it. "I am not finished revising, but I promise I'll have it for you before you leave."

"Deal. And I will give you your next book suggestion right after." Paige decided she'd better add an asterisk to that last statement. "That is assuming it's okay with your dad."

"I'm sure it will be, but you can ask him if you like." Lucy stopped in front of a closed door. "There are two bedrooms downstairs, in addition to the common room, the library, the kitchen, and the dining room. This bedroom's mine." Lucy again looked at Paige. She was trying to put to rest her fear that she was boring Paige to death. "Do you want to see it?"

Paige remembered what it was like to be eleven and to think of your room as the crown jewel of all your earthly possessions. It was in her bedroom that she first began to idolize authors and books. "I would love to see it."

Lucy opened the door to her room and then moved to the side to allow a better view. Paige immediately noticed the posters in her room. They were all from movies which started their existence as books. In the center of the room, directly in front of the doorway, stood a four-foot-wide bookcase that ran nearly the entire height of the wall, from the floor to within a foot and a half of the ceiling. As it stood there this evening, Paige guessed the bookcase was ninety percent full. Lucy was telling the truth. Her father had been taking her to the bookstore every week for several years. Paige approached the books. "Impressive collection, Lucy."

Lucy beamed as though Paige had named her the reader of the year for the entire state of New Hampshire. She was proud of herself for both the quantity and the quality of the books she read. It made her happy Paige validated these opinions. "Thank you." Lucy noticed Paige's gaze landed on the black and white eight and a half by eleven picture, which hung to the right of her bookshelf and overtop her bed. "That's a picture of my mom."

Paige stepped closer to the picture. "Wow, she's very pretty."

"Thanks." Lucy frowned. There never seemed to be an easy way to let people know her mother had died. It always felt to Lucy like the moment when strangers found out ended all conversation, like it sucked the room dry of air. At least, the air-sucking hypothesis was the best explanation she could come up with for why no one could ever find any words after she told them. "I don't think she looks like me." Lucy paused. If she didn't get it out of the way now, it would get more and more awkward as time passed. She knew it was better to get it over with, so she hurriedly added in one dismissive burst, "She died four years ago."

Paige instantly turned around and enveloped Lucy in another hug. This one was big. It was spontaneous. It came from somewhere deep within her, and she had no control over it. "I am so sorry for you, Lucy. That is horrible. Absolutely horrible."

Lucy was surprised by this reaction. No grownup had ever done anything other than get quiet when they found out about her mom. It made her like Paige about a thousand times more than she did before she knew. The fact she started from a point of near idolization did not have an effect on the thousand-times figure. Paige just passed Ian as her second favorite person. "I'm okay. It was four years ago." That was Lucy's stock response. She gave it now because she always gave it. It was a means toward making the situation less awkward. She gave it to Paige because habit left her with nothing else to offer.

Paige broke the hug but was having none of Lucy's rationalizations. "You don't have to pretend for me. Four years is no wrinkle in time, Lucy. Besides, if you don't mind my saying so, I think you look exactly like your mother."

Lucy's smile bloomed again. "You really think so?"

"You two could be twins." Paige would have said it either way, to make Lucy feel better about those four years, but, fortunately for her, it was also true.

"I'm so happy you're here this Christmas, Paige."

"I'm happy to be here." Again, Paige would have said this either way but, for the third time in a row, that which was intended to make Lucy feel better turned out to be true as well. If Ian, Eli, and Lucy were any indication, the town of Dayton, New Hampshire, was the best-kept secret in the United States. She would do what she had to do when it came to her critique of Christmas in Dayton. It would be a whole lot easier a confection to make because of how wonderful the people here were. "Shall we go outside and finish the tour?"

Lucy tried to be a considerate guide, just the way her father taught her. "If you don't think you will be too cold."

Paige entertained this for a moment. "Will it be warmer tomorrow?"

Lucy laughed. "It probably won't be warmer until March."

"Then let's do it now." Paige said decisively as she put on her coat and gloves.

Lucy got her winter things from the closet by the

front door. She then led Paige outside to the path which surrounded the lake. She put her tour guide demeanor back on as she prepared to detail more facts about their surroundings. "Lake Winnipesaukee is the largest lake in New Hampshire."

"Really." Paige was genuinely impressed. "I didn't know that."

Lucy continued with sincere satisfaction. "It's true. It has a length of just under twenty-one miles and, in some places, it is over nine miles wide. It is also the third-largest lake in all of New England."

Paige thought the irrational pride Lucy was taking in the lake which filled up her backyard was adorable. She wanted very much to keep her going. "What else can you tell me?"

Lucy had been waiting for this invitation. She knew two things about this lake Paige would love because they were about other authors. "Well, Thornton Wilder mentions the lake in his play Our Town."

Paige pursed her lips and pointed her index finger at Lucy, a sign of appreciation of the trivia. "I'll have to go back and reread that now."

"And then one more thing." Lucy could tell Paige was interested in the facts she was listing about her lake. This had the effect of making her talk about them with the surpassing pride she actually felt for them.

Lucy was correct. Paige wasn't faking interest. Not only did she like Lucy, but she was also happy to get this information about the lake. It would help her later when she went to write the next show for her podcast. Of course, she could Google the lake and get the same facts.

But it was better to know which facts were important to the locals. Especially when the locals were only eleven years old. Facts which stuck in the mind of an eleven-year-old were always the best kind of facts. "Lay it on me, Lucy."

"Parts of the movie On Golden Pond were filmed here." Lucy once again beamed with pride over her lake.

Paige was skeptical. Not about the accuracy, but about that movie being one an eleven-year-old would be familiar with. "You've seen that?"

"Yep." Lucy took as much pride in having seen the movie as she did in the fact that her lake had been in the movie.

"And you liked it?" Paige contained her doubt with difficulty.

"I thought it was a sweet story." Lucy wasn't sure if she'd made her first misstep with Paige. She attempted to clarify. "Why, do you not like it?"

"Oh no, I love it. It just seems like it could be a little slow, that's all." Paige turned to face Lucy, who stopped beside a small cottage on the banks of the lake.

"I guess it is a little slow, but I love the way Norman ends up caring for Billy." Lucy switched her attention to the cottage behind them. Talking about the movie got her out on that dangerous cliff of emotions about her mom. She did not want to go there. Why did this keep happening with Paige? It would not do, not right now, for her to tell Paige that On Golden Pond was one of her mom's favorite movies. That's why she changed the subject to the cabin behind her. "There are three of these little cottages on the property. My Dad and Ian built all three of them. My Mom helped with the first two. I helped a lot with the last one."

"I bet the last one is the best." Paige offered.

"It probably is." Lucy tried for a moment to pretend as though she were capable of a narcissism that would assume a project she had been involved with would be the best, but she couldn't maintain a straight face. "Of course, the fact that it has the largest Jacuzzi might have something to do with it. People always seem to love that."

Lucy walked back toward the main house. Paige followed beside her. "You should come to dinner with us tonight."

Paige felt she must give a customary objection. She did, however, repeat that trick she used earlier by phrasing it in a way that was unique to the budding relationship she was developing with Lucy. "That's as sweet as Norman's feelings for Billy, but I wouldn't want to impose on your father."

"He already said I could invite you. As long as I also invited Jessica and Ian. He said to be sure and tell you he didn't mind at all." Lucy was several moves ahead of Paige when it came to eliminating obstacles in the form of customary objections. "Also, don't worry, he always makes a ton of food."

"Of course, I will come then." Paige pulled out her phone. "Let me text Jessica so she knows not to pick up anything for us on her way back from the rental car agency."

Paige took a moment to complete this action on her phone. While she did this, she couldn't help thinking of the way Lucy said Eli spoke of the dinner invitation.

'Make sure,' he had said. Did that mean he really wanted her to come? Or was he just being nice? The problem with being an English major, other than being gifted an overly complex set of ethical maxims, was a propensity for parsing words for their deeper meanings. Sometimes, a rose was a rose was a rose.

Lucy's face strained to contain her smile. She was so happy. It was becoming a state of being when she was with Paige. She loved that they would get to spend more time together this evening. The feeling of joy led her to an overwhelming question. She couldn't help asking it. "What do you think of this place so far, Paige?"

Paige enveloped the lake and the surrounding woods in the declining sunlight in a big imaginary bear hug. "I think this place is supernaturally beautiful. It's almost like stepping into a painting." Paige directed her gaze from the landscape to the eleven-year-old girl walking beside her. "But without a doubt, the best part has been the people. Your dad, Ian, you. Especially you, have made me feel welcome from the moment I got here." Paige blurted this next part out without fully reviewing it beforehand. "It's been like coming home." Once it was out there, settling on the snow-covered path which led back to the main house, it felt accurate. Paige wondered if it hadn't been a little much, just the same. She was glad Eli hadn't been there to hear her say it.

"I hope we change your mind about Christmas." An impish grin spread across Lucy's face. It reminded Paige of an expression she had seen Eli make earlier. "If anyone can do it, it's my Dad. He should be crowned King Christmas or something. That's how much he gets into it." Lucy stopped herself short. She was about to reveal something she didn't want to reveal just yet, not even to her new hero, Paige Langford.

Paige let a bit of harmless fake sarcasm infect her voice. "Really, there are so few Christmas decorations up, I would never have guessed he was such a fan."

Lucy laughed. "If you think it's bad now, just wait until we get to the actual day."

Paige's fake sarcasm exited. It was replaced by genuine doubt or, perhaps, awe. "You mean he's not done yet?

Lucy stopped on the steps leading back up to the porch of the main house. She did this because she didn't want to talk about her Dad, and his obsession with Christmas, where he might hear her. It wasn't because she was embarrassed by him. Nor was it because she had been infected by the anti-Christmas sentiment Paige offered in her five reasons for disliking Christmas podcast, as her Dad suspected. It was because she was afraid she might tear up. She loved what her Dad did to get ready for Christmas.

"He's not even close to done. He adds one new thing to each room for every day in December leading up to Christmas Eve. And then on Christmas Eve, he really lets loose." Lucy laughed with pleasure as she thought about her Dad letting loose with the Christmas spirit.

"Wow." This impressed Paige. She had a hard time imagining how anyone could add more decorations to what was already in her room. She felt confident that if Santa Claus ever had reindeer troubles and needed a place to stay for the night, he would be happy in her room in its current state.

“Dad believes part of the Christmas spirit comes from seeing it all around you.” Lucy had heard her father’s philosophizing about Christmas spirit nearly as often as she heard him give the tour of the house and the lake. She knew it by rote. The same way she knew his tour guide speech by rote.

“I admit, that’s not a bad theory.” Paige looked at Lucy while considering the theory’s application in the real world. “It feels as though my Grinchy heart has grown a size or two just since I’ve been talking with you.” Paige started up the porch stairs. Her Grinchy heart comment was as much of an admission that Eli’s Christmas spirit theory had any merit as she was prepared to allow in this moment. “Now, let’s get back inside so we can both warm up.”

Lucy bounded in the door like the eleven-year-old she was. Paige turned and took a minute to drink in the beauty of this lakefront property in the diminishing December light. The snow looked fresh, even though it fell several days before, because the cold air and lack of direct sunlight were enmeshed in a conspiracy to make this winter scene as beautiful as possible. Paige thought it would be heavenly to live here surrounded by this much nature every day. Los Angeles had been good to her. It was her city. But nothing in LA was ever as beautiful as Eli’s front porch was in that moment.

Paige’s mini-reverie concluded when Lucy bumped the screen door back open and poked her head outside. “You coming?”

Paige turned away from the beauty of nature and into the beauty of precocious adolescence. She wasn’t sure which one she appreciated more. “Right behind you.

Just wanted to get one more look at Thornton Wilder's lake." This time, Paige followed Lucy.

CHAPTER FIVE

Rigid, the skeleton of habit alone upholds the human frame.

Paige was upstairs slowly going through more of the emails from the fans of her show. It was her way of obeying Woolf's mantra about skeletons being upheld by habits. Her attention to the habitual task was half-hearted at best. She made her way through five responses when she elected to close the lid on her computer. She wanted to engage with her audience, but she couldn't keep herself from thinking about Eli and his magnificent daughter. She felt that those who had taken time out of their lives to send her a note thanking her for some aspect of her show deserved better than a distracted span of attention.

Even, Paige conceded, those that emailed her to start an argument about why Christmas was the greatest day ever invented by humanity. Even those people deserved better than her half-hearted attention. Just because they were wrong, didn't mean she should answer them when her mind was focused on other things. And why, she wondered, was her mind so focused on those other things? First, she had felt an irresistible pull of human gravity in Eli's direction from the moment she met him. After that, Lucy captivated her with her adorable charm. They were like a one-two punch of small-town New Hampshire Americana. Paige thought, and realized the idea might count as irony, they would make great characters in a story. How would they feel, though, when they learned Paige was in their lives as an author and not a friend? Why couldn't she be friends with them and make characters of them at the same time? Didn't most novelists do exactly that? Would it really be so bad if she allowed their love of Christmas into her own heart? This cross-examination of herself and her motives progressed no further. There was another knock on her bedroom door. Paige felt like she was having Deja-vu. "Who is it?" She asked.

"It's me." Jessica responded. "Can I come in?"

Paige opened the door. "Of course, you can." She crossed over and took a seat at the foot of her bed, leaving the chair open for Jessica. "What's up? Did you get the car?"

"Yes, I got the car. But who cares about the car?" Jessica threw her head back. "I am moving here. Literally."

"What?" Paige was so confused.

"Ian! Did you even see Ian?" Jessica shook her head at the sheer inconceivability of Ian. "I think I'm in love." Paige studied her best friend's full-body conviction —the head tilt, the half-smile, the unapologetic rush of certainty. That was the thing about Jessica. She didn't dabble in feelings, she declared them. Paige didn't always understand it, but she admired the abandon.

"Really. You just met him." Paige let her voice riddle with doubt. "You know how you sometimes..." Paige searched for an appropriate word. "You tend to over...

estimate." It was the most neutral word she could come up with.

Jessica fired back with theatrical indignation. "Oh no, don't do that, Paige. You can't be hitting me in the face with all your overly rationalized inability to believe in anything you can't describe in ten words or less."

Paige blinked, then smirked. That line—flung from somewhere deep in Jessica's spontaneous truth vault, was annoyingly accurate. It was Jessica in pure form. She was fearless in emotional language, unapologetic in confrontation, quick with the kind of phrasing that left Paige briefly speechless. Jessica, as was her way, had once again hit the nail directly on the head. "I love that. And I think you're right. I do refuse to believe in anything that can't be summarized in ten words or less. Thank you for the insight. However, it doesn't change the fact that you tend to inflate the positive qualities of those you are attracted to."

"Yeah, but what I'm trying to get you to appreciate is that, *in this case*, I am not inflating. Ian is wildly good-looking *and* a really kind, decent guy too."

Paige saw Jessica wasn't just framing a pitch. It was a plea. She recognized the pattern. When Jessica cared, she needed Paige to agree. Not for validation exactly, but for confirmation. Paige knew she was Jessica's arbiter of character, radar of red flags, patron saint of rational caution. On the other hand, Paige knew just as well what her silence could do. A single raised brow from her had once dismantled an entire summer crush. She didn't want to be the reason this one unraveled, especially not when Jessica seemed so... sure. Still, there was no way she could agree that Jessica could be certain Ian was all the things Jessica thought he was from vanishingly small amount of time Jessica had known him. Caution guided her response. "You learned this in the hour it took you to drive to town, pick up the rental car, and come back."

"I think I learned it this afternoon in the three minutes it took for him to drive us from the bottom of the driveway to the top in Eli's SUV." Paige watched as Jessica reconsidered her avenue of attack. Jessica wasn't above winning approval by changing the rules of engagement. "Speaking of Eli, you two kind of hit it off, didn't you?"

Paige mulled this statement over for a moment. It upset her that Jessica picked up on what she thought was only in her mind. On the one hand, it meant she wasn't being as inconspicuous about her feelings as she should be. On the other hand, it intrigued her. Jessica had phrased her question in the jargon of mutual attraction. She said, 'You two kind of hit it off'. About that part, Paige wanted to talk more. "Yes. I can't speak for him, obviously. But I do feel something." Paige frowned because she couldn't name the feeling. "I don't know what it is. I'm not sure I want to find out any more about what it is either." Paige erupted with a finality meant to convince her own wavering will. "We don't have time for this!" Now that she had herself in line, she repeated the same idea while also including Jessica in the target. "Neither of us has time for this. We are leaving in a few days."

"Yes, but..."

Paige wasn't interested in more discussion. "No 'buts', Jessica. If either of us pursue anything beyond mild friendship, it can only end in hurt feelings. Probably on both sides."

"People have long-distance relationships, Paige."

Paige recognized the familiar glint in her friend's eyes. Jessica wasn't arguing because she disagreed. She was arguing because the idea mattered to her. That refusal to surrender her heart to statistics was exactly what made her Jessica. And deep down, Paige respected her for it. Unfortunately for Jessica, Ian, and even Eli, she had convinced herself of the wisdom of her own advice. All that remained was to push relentlessly on her point, like a general in pursuit of a crippling battlefield defeat. Her extemporaneous response was a perfect reversal of the argument Jessica had used back in Los Angeles over the takeout food from China One. "Are you going to move to New Hampshire?"

Even before Jessica answered, Paige knew what she was going to say. "No. I'm not."

Paige delivered the natural follow-up. "Do you believe there is any chance he is going to move to Los Angeles?"

"No, I don't." Jessica sighed as part of her surrendered. "I get it. I really do."

"Then what's the problem?" Sometimes Paige really struggled to understand why people pursued feelings which weren't productive. Something very close to that idea was, at its core, the sum total of her entire philosophy against Christmas. As Jessica had just laid out in the form of a linguistic law, it could also be summed up in ten words or less.

Jessica glared at Paige, annoyed by having to say it out loud. "Have you looked at him? He's like all the best parts of a cross between Robert Redford and Brad Pitt."

Paige laughed out loud. "Start thinking with your brain and stop thinking with your eyes, and everything will work out just fine." Paige glanced at her phone to check the time. "We should head down to dinner." She stood to signify that the conversation was over. She wouldn't tolerate any more silly ideas that revolved around the two of them in any way associated with the two men they recently met from the town of Dayton, New Hampshire.

Jessica stood as well. She looked to Paige like a petulant child who had been told she couldn't have another cookie. "Alright. Okay. I get it. And you're right." Jessica eyed Paige with mock distaste. "Are you happy now that I am miserable?"

"I am happy now that you are agreeing to be miserably reasonable." Paige walked out the door of her room, followed closely by a 'miserable' Jessica.

§

Eli put the finishing touches on the meal he had prepared for Ian and his new guests. While he did this, Lucy told him all about her conversation with Paige from when she gave her a tour of the property. He could tell his daughter was invested in Paige at a level which seemed odd given how long they had known each other. Now was the time to discover what was causing this outsized interest. Fortunately for him, the saffron and rice needed a few more minutes to simmer. "Lucy, can I ask you something?"

"Of course, Dad."

"First, did you get all the place settings down?" Eli decided to start with something light. Get the ball rolling, then ease into the harder questions.

Eli smiled as Lucy answered, "Yep. I used my own judgment and went with the snowman set." He could hear the satisfaction tucked inside her voice. The way her voice crested into a little rise, then nestled beneath a confident delivery. She hadn't asked. She hadn't double-checked. And that, more than the accuracy of her choice, mattered to him. Intellectual self-reliance was something he'd quietly tried to model to her for years. Watching her flex those muscles in such a simple, domestic moment hit him deeper than any declaration of love she could give.

"Excellent. You know those are my favorite." Eli looked at his daughter, trying to figure out the safest way to broach this subject. He didn't know what was causing his daughter's interest in Paige, but he was limited to the five more minutes the rice needed to simmer to find out. Perhaps it might be better to wait until this evening, when he told her goodnight, to ask what was going on. Eli stirred the rice with practiced ease, pretending not to notice how closely Lucy was watching him. But of course she saw it. That fractional shift in his posture, that momentary pause before his reply. She had a knack for catching tension mid-breath.

"What's up, Dad?"

As always, Lucy forced his hand, not out of defiance, but as part of the subtle empathy she wielded like a superpower. Eli glanced at the pot, then back at her. His original estimation was off by a smidge, he still had five minutes. Maybe that was enough time to try. Or maybe the fact that she'd asked meant she already knew.

What a perceptive kid he had. She could always tell the moment he was perplexed or bothered. She really was just like Anna when it came to sensing his moods. He would try. "Can I ask you about something I can't explain?"

Lucy put her palms together and then opened them. "Open book, Dad. You know that."

It was a thing they had developed after her mom died. Eli wanted something visual to use whenever he felt Lucy might be holding her sadness up inside her. It was, in other words, an invitation to talk as well as permission to say whatever was on her mind. Since her mother loved books as much as Eli, it seemed a natural bit of symbolism for the two of them to use.

Eli performed the pantomime too, along with the incantation. "Open book," he said. He then gathered himself to ask the question that was really on his mind. "It seems like you hold Paige in high esteem."

Lucy offered the obvious. "That's because she's such a nice person, Dad."

"Well, granted, so far, she seems like a very fine person." Eli wasn't sure if he wanted to cast aspersions on Paige by reminding Lucy people weren't always what they seemed. Doing so, he thought, would be much more about winning a point than having a discussion. Besides, he was pretty sure himself; Paige was a great person. It occurred to him he might be able to steer the conversation indirectly toward Lucy's fascination with Paige by first detouring through the land of her, unknown to him before today, desire to become a writer when she grew up. "Is it the fact that she's a writer? Is that why she's so interesting to you?"

"She did write that series of books I was into

this summer." Lucy egged her father's memory on, "You remember. The ones we got from Mr. Waller's shop the week after school let out."

Whoa. That one hit Eli like a smack in the face. He remembered the series *now*. If he squinted really hard in his imagination, he almost thought he could remember Paige's name under the title. Things were starting to make sense. At least he felt more confident Lucy's infatuation wasn't derived from the anti-Christmas podcast. He breathed a sigh of relief. Still, he had to deal with the fact that he should have been much better prepared for Paige's visit than he had been. In a way he wouldn't soon let go of, it felt like he had let Lucy down. "Yeah, I do remember the series." Eli looked at his daughter so she would know he wasn't trying to make excuses. "To be honest, though, I hadn't put two and two together. I didn't know she was the author of the books, Lucy. I'm sorry about that."

Eli nodded slowly, but her apology still tugged at him. He should've known. Should've paid closer attention. It felt like a quiet miss. One he didn't want to admit lingered beneath the surface. But Lucy wasn't dwelling. Her voice was light, almost amused. "Don't worry about it, Dad. I don't expect you to read every book I read. That would be silly."

It surprised him how quickly she moved past it. How firmly she placed the whole thing back into perspective. Paige's books, Lucy had explained, were in a completely different league than those horse-girl stories she'd breezed through the previous winter and spring. She wasn't holding him accountable for oversight. She was reassuring him. Eli exhaled. Maybe she was learning something bigger than just literary taste. Something in the neighborhood of how to be a good person. "Still, if it was that important to you, I should have read them. I *definitely wish* I had read them before she got here."

"Well, I can recommend you read her books. They are very good. But I doubt Paige minds you didn't. They're not written for grownups."

"So, that series is why you have this new desire to be a writer." Eli wanted to talk about this even more than he wanted to talk about Paige. The fact that she never mentioned it made him nervous about what other things she might not want to tell him about.

"That's part of it," she said. "I have definitely gotten into the idea of being a writer." Eli watched as Lucy grimaced, as though she were coming across an idea that was sour to her personality. "I'm sorry I hadn't talked about that with you, Dad."

Eli didn't need Lucy apologizing to him. He wasn't the sort of dad who was going to require he know everything going on in her life. He wanted to stop that train before it had a chance to leave the station. "Oh no, sweetheart, please don't worry about that. You're getting older now. I'm sure there will be more and more things you choose to keep to yourself. All I need you to know is that I am always here for you no matter what." He paused for a moment, letting the perfect way to express his sentiment build. "I just want you to know you don't have to tell me everything, but you can always tell me anything."

Lucy smiled. "I love that. And I believe it too. I know you will always be there for me."

Eli turned his attention to the stove. It was time to deal with the saffron and rice or it would be overcooked. He removed the pot from the burner and turned off the heat. He then split the brown rice between five plates and removed the grilled chicken from where it had been keeping warm in the oven. He placed a piece of chicken on top of the rice on each of the five plates and then turned to his daughter. "If you can carry two plates, I can get the other three. The other sides are already on the table."

Lucy grabbed two plates and headed toward the swinging doors which cordoned off the kitchen from the rest of the house. She stopped before going through. Eli sensed there was something she wanted him to know. The look on her face said she needed him to know it right *then*, so it wouldn't become any more of an issue. "The story I wrote. The one Aunt Teresa liked so much..."

Eli balanced two plates on his left forearm while carrying the odd plate in his right hand. "Yeah?"

"It was about Mom. Not in any obvious way, but anyone who knows us would know." Lucy glanced at the floor. "That's why I didn't want to tell you about it. It was kind of about how I still miss her." Lucy let it all tumble out of her in one rapid burst, like ripping off a Band-Aid. "I didn't want you to think you were letting me down somehow because I still miss her sometimes."

"I'm sure it's amazing." Eli watched his daughter's face brighten at the compliment. "I'd love to read it whenever, or if ever, you want to share it with me."

"Thanks Dad. You're the best." Lucy disappeared through the swinging doors.

Eli watched the doors sway at opposing intervals.

He took a minute to compose himself as the friction in the hinges slowed the doors to motionlessness. He felt a certain kinship with the doors in that moment. As though all the energy in his body had been sapped out of him by a rigorous force. There certainly was no limit on the amount of time a young girl could miss her mother, but that thought didn't make it any easier for Eli to handle. He shook his head. A physical reminder for his body to focus on the dinner which he had prepared. He then walked through the swinging doors with a renewed commitment to make sure his daughter had everything she needed. He would start by making this Christmas, The Best Christmas Ever.

Eli arrived in the dining room to find all his guests seated. Lucy placed the two plates she carried in front of Paige and Jessica. Eli followed this up by giving one to Ian, one to Lucy, and then setting the last one down in front of his chair at the head of the table. He started with an apology. "It doesn't look like much, but hopefully it tastes better than it looks."

Ian leaned in conspiratorially toward Paige and Jessica. "Trust me, it tastes outstanding."

Not to be outdone, Lucy also took the opportunity to brag on her father. "Dad cooks the simplest things, but they always taste so good."

Eli didn't like the praise. It wasn't his style. "Okay, okay. Let these two Angel City Dwellers decide for themselves. Dig in." Everyone picked up a fork and knife at the same time. As they began to cut into their food, Eli permitted himself one small bout of boasting. He did this because he didn't want Paige and Jessica to worry about their appetites. "Although, even if you don't enjoy the dinner, I can tell you with confidence the breakfast in the morning will be delicious. I've never had anyone stay here that couldn't find something they enjoyed at our breakfast table." The sound of knives and forks clanking was the only sound in the dining room for the next several seconds.

Paige was the first to speak up. "This is delicious."

Jessica immediately followed. She wasn't finished chewing when she spoke. She gave the praise around the food in her mouth. "Oh my, that's an understatement."

Ian managed to get in on the gratitude pileup before Eli could call an end to it. "I told you two, Eli is a master in the kitchen."

Eli smiled. He loved cooking. He loved it more when others enjoyed the fruits of his labor. "You all are too kind." Of course, as much as he loved it when people appreciated his cooking, he hated it when the skill he possessed for cooking made him the center of attention. He determined to change the subject so that he wouldn't have to continue to be embarrassed by a flood of compliments. "What do you two have planned for tomorrow?"

Paige looked at Jessica. Jessica shrugged her shoulders. "We have to meet Mr. Turner in the morning at ten, but other than that, we are open to suggestions," Paige offered.

Jessica picked up the thread, frank and efficient in a way Eli now recognized as her trademark. "I'd say we're in need of suggestions." Classic Jessica, he thought. Paige seemed to agree. Eli caught the flicker of recognition in her eyes before Lucy spoke up.

"I have one," she said. "Although, it would be for tonight."

Paige paused mid-bite. "Let's hear it."

Eli watched Lucy shift slightly in her seat, gathering confidence. "Well, you two are here because the mayor challenged you not to be overwhelmed by Dayton's Christmas spirit, right?" She summarized the public terms of the bet neatly, in that brisk, composed way she'd inherited from Anna.

"That's right," Paige said.

Jessica again refused to be in need of convincing. "Let the records show I am not lacking in Christmas spirit."

Paige rolled her eyes and deadpanned like it was an old routine. "Jessica's feelings about Christmas spirit are noted, for the three hundred and seventh time, in the permanent record." Eli couldn't resist a slight smile at the pair Paige and Jessica made. What a wonderful relationship. They were like an old married couple with a private shorthand that somehow got baked into every remark. Paige turned her attention back to Lucy. "What were you thinking, Lucy?"

"Dad and I have a tradition," she said, glancing at Eli. "Every year we make an ornament or a decoration. This time we settled on popcorn garland for all the trees in all the rooms."

Eli caught the unspoken question in her eyes and stepped in, ready with an exit ramp if his guests looked too weary. "They might be too jet-lagged for that, Lucy. They were on a red-eye flight last night after all."

Jessica didn't hesitate. "I won't answer for Paige,

but in my thirty-five years I've never made popcorn garland, and I'd love to end that streak tonight."

Eli registered the genuine enthusiasm in her voice. It didn't feel like politeness—it felt like curiosity. Then Ian chimed in with a neutrality which tried too hard to be camouflage. "I could be up for that too, if you didn't mind another pair of hands, Eli." Ian's glance at Jessica as he said this affirmed he was never going to win any acting awards. Eli saw the way Jessica looked back at him. There was encouragement in her eyes. What in the world was going on this Christmas? Eli let himself absorb the circumstances a moment longer before responding. The garland invitation wasn't just festive filler. It was Lucy being Lucy. She was offering these new people in her life a chance at connection. She was doing this the way only an adolescent can, with no trace of agenda. Eli had let the moment hang long enough. It was time to just have fun. "You're always welcome, Ian. Don't be silly." Despite the peace offering, Eli couldn't resist poking a little fun at his best friend's interest in Jessica. "Although it has to be the first time you've ever *wanted* to join us for garland making."

Eli watched as Ian tried to cover his tracks. He knew Ian was as bashful as he was good-looking and kind. It would take him another day or so before he could publicly face up to his recent crush without turning red in both his cheeks. "I'm just hoping to make it harder on Paige over there to keep believing Dayton won't convert her into being as big a fan of Christmas as we all are."

Eli looked at Paige. He thought about how, in that moment, she looked as lovely as any person could look. She was one of those people who wore their beauty with ease. Her natural blonde hair fell slightly past her shoulder where it gently curled over her crisp black shirt. The Christmas lights he strung around the mantle mixed with the blue in her eyes to give a palette of colors an impressionist would fawn over. She looked so beautiful in this house, sitting at his table, he got lost in the moment and asked her to join in, even though he had intended to be strong and wait for her to volunteer. "What do you say? You up for some popcorn garland making fun, Paige?"

Paige scanned the table slowly, absorbing everyone's quiet expectation. Eli watched her wrestle with it—if you could call it wrestling. What he saw instead was surrender. Not to pressure, but to the strangely magnetic certainty that this mattered. That the garland, ridiculous or not, had its place in the balance of things. "How could I resist?" she said.

In the pause that followed, Eli noticed something shift behind her eyes. Whatever had come to her in that moment wasn't about decorations or Dayton anymore. It was deeper. Eli was becoming increasingly positive that something about Dayton, New Hampshire, was really getting to her. Why did that thought thrill him?

CHAPTER SIX

To love makes one solitary.

Those words rolled around inside Paige's head as she pressed snooze on her alarm clock. She was having a dream in which Virginia Woolf, the one from the first page of a Google Images search, was berating her with the words from her novel, Mrs. Dalloway. Virginia was doing this because she knew Paige had been having romantic thoughts about Eli Ryder. She had to hit the snooze button twice before she was finally able to keep her eyes open longer than the minimum time it took to reflexively find her phone and silence that incredibly annoying noise for good. If not for the taunting presence of Virginia Woolf over the content of her dreamscape, she might have continued hitting snooze indefinitely.

Ordinarily, she was someone who got up at the time she set her alarm. The inclination to push snooze, which Virginia Woolf successfully subverted, was a reaction caused by the time zone troubles switching coasts in a single day caused her. In fact, she thought she might need an ibuprofen or two if the dull ringing in her head didn't subside after she forced herself out of bed. It had been three o'clock East Coast time when she last remembered looking at the clock. The midnight flight from Los Angeles to New Hampshire two nights before hadn't done her any favors either. She hadn't slept more than four hours of the time it took to get to New Hampshire. Those four hours had been fitful at best. On top of this, she also forgot to set the coffee to automatically brew at the time she wanted to wake up. It was probably that fact which convinced her to quit staring at the ceiling and get out of bed. She knew her body too well to risk depriving it of sleep *and* caffeine.

As her feet hit the floor, her thoughts drifted back to her night with the Ryders. The popcorn garland making had been a tremendous hit with all of them. Jessica claimed she didn't remember the last time she had that much fun. Paige was pretty sure this was due to Ian's inability to thread the needle through the popcorn without breaking the individual pieces unless Jessica was standing beside him, holding his hands, as he did it. The two seemed to be in an unwritten conspiracy to see if they could flirt with each other as much as possible while still maintaining they weren't flirting with each other at all.

Lucy had been an absolute joy to be around. She was practically an expert in the popcorn garland making field, and Eli let her play the instructor role for all the popcorn garland making novices who were staying in her house. She relished the opportunity to finally be the teacher after so many years as a student. And then there was Eli... The connection between the two of them was unmistakable.

Lucy's bedtime was nine o'clock on school nights, so that had been the official end of the evening. Ian went home. Jessica retired to her room. Eli protested about having a big day coming up. Paige complained about her jet lag and lack of sleep on her red-eye flight. The pair shook hands, formally, in Eli's living room, surrounded by a sea of popcorn strung together with cranberries. After which, Paige went to her room while Eli locked up the house and then went to his. The house was still and quiet… not a creature was stirring kind of quiet.

By a stroke of luck, or perhaps fate, they met in the kitchen twenty-five minutes later. Paige was in search of a glass to fill with water and keep beside her bed in case she woke up thirsty. Eli got up because, in all the popcorn stringing excitement, he forgot to make Lucy's lunch for her final day of school before Christmas break. Eli turned the light on in the kitchen, and Paige appeared a half-second later. The pair then spent the ensuing three hours talking about everything from politics, where their views were in fair agreement, to the novels of William Faulkner, where their views were miles apart.

Paige waited by the coffeepot in her room for her first cup to finish brewing as she thought back on how much fun those three hours had been. The popcorn garland making by itself was great and would make a good backstory for her next podcast, but the talk with Eli was exceptional. Paige had never had such a visceral connection with another human being. It wasn't just the outrageous attraction she felt toward him that motivated her either. Much like Jessica claimed to feel about Ian, Eli was to Paige one of the kindest, most charming, most attractive men she had ever met. Of course, Paige couldn't forget that just yesterday she had called Jessica out for saying out loud about Ian exactly what she was now thinking about Eli. She couldn't let herself be inconsistent. She had to limit the time she spent with him because, at this point, she knew she couldn't trust herself to be rational.

Unfortunately, before their three-hour talk ended, Paige learned Eli was supposed to meet with the mayor directly after Paige's scheduled meeting with him. Naturally, they made plans to ride into town together. Paige wasn't worried about the drive because Jessica would be there to dampen the attraction she felt toward Eli by being an unwitting physical reminder Paige was from Los Angeles. Her job, her house, and her life were all in Los Angeles. She couldn't think about entering into anything other than friendship with someone who lived three thousand miles away from her. Especially when that someone was a widowed father raising an eleven-year-old daughter.

Paige blew into her coffee in order to cool it down. She thought about running downstairs to grab a couple of ice cubes from the fridge but didn't want to risk seeing Eli while she was wearing her pajamas. She took the cup over to the window and set it on the sill. She figured that was the coldest place in the room and, therefore, the place most likely to suck some of the warmth from her cup. She opened her laptop and logged into her email account in order to work down the number not read. By continually sifting through as many as she could squeeze in here and there over the course of the last few weeks, she had winnowed the total unopened well below fifty. Her goal was to get it to zero before Christmas Day.

Out of the corner of her eye, she saw Eli's SUV heading up the driveway toward the house. This caught her attention, so she refocused her gaze on the beautiful winter scene outside her window. She saw Lucy's school bus retreating through the snow-covered branches of the trees which nestled up close to the highway. She admired Eli for his dedication to his daughter and his secondary dedication to his business. He seemed to be doing an amazing job of managing both roles. If there were some way to nominate him for an award for his efforts, she would do it. Unfortunately, parenting didn't come with an awards show, and his bed-and-breakfast was already listed as one of the ten best in the state of New Hampshire. There was little she could do for him in terms of recognition.

Paige shut the lid on her laptop, having only taken five messages out of unread status. She wanted to get a shower so she could go down to the breakfast Eli said would be so good yesterday evening during dinner. The emails would still be there later. The breakfast wouldn't be. Besides, they had made those plans to travel to the mayor's office together. Second impressions were almost as important as first impressions. She didn't want Eli believing she was one of those who didn't show up for things on time.

Thinking of her meeting with Vincent caused her more anxiety. Eli explained to her last night that he would be seeing Vincent today to pitch him his idea for a Christmas Eve Carnival on the ice of Lake Winnipesauke. It was when Eli suggested they go in to see Vincent together to save time that Paige's anxiety spiked. With Eli there, she wouldn't be able to speak freely about the dishonest parts of her Christmas adventure in Dayton. That would make for a second impression she could never erase. She wanted to rid herself of these shaky feelings but couldn't until she found a way to rid herself of the dishonesty.

Still, the idea of spending time with Eli was equal parts exhilarating and discomforting. She didn't know how to exit this merry-go-round of feelings. It wasn't something she had experienced before. Her inclination to be rational and clear-headed, the part of her that always won any disagreements she had with the more emotional parts of herself, was being weak in its objection to 'falling for' Eli. Yes, her superego was technically doing its job in pointing out the futility of pursuing any strengthening of her feelings. But no, it wasn't providing her with the usual ironclad ultimatum she required. There were, in other words, no teeth in its prohibition. As she made her way to the enormous private bathroom in her room, she wondered why this fact didn't bother her. Why, she wondered, did she look forward to seeing Eli more than anything else she would do that day?

§

Thirty minutes later, Paige was seated sweetly at the big table in Eli's dining room, waiting for breakfast. The Cookes, a married couple in their fifties with no children, were the only other guests at the bed-and-breakfast that morning. This was no commentary on the quality of the bed-and-breakfast, but rather a reflection of the fact that it was a Thursday, and it was less than three days until Christmas. Paige made intermittent small talk with Mrs. Cooke while they all waited for Eli and his nineteen-year-old kitchen helper, Ross, to finish cooking breakfast. Mr. Cooke read stories on his phone about his favorite team, the New England Patriots.

An avid follower of true-crime podcasts, Mrs. Cooke was familiar with the medium and pledged to give Paige and Jessica's show a chance as soon as she got back to the cabin later that morning. Paige could tell Mrs. Cooke was having a hard time digesting the reasons she and Jessica were staying at Eli's bed-and-breakfast. "You mean the town flew you in, and put you up in this wonderful bed-and-breakfast, all free of charge?" Incredulous hardly did justice to Mrs. Cooke's tone.

Paige could tell she hadn't explained it well enough the first time, so she tried again. "Well, our podcast is very highly rated. I think the mayor believes the publicity alone will be worth it. He sees it as a long-range form of advertising for the area."

"But he's also betting you will change your mind based on your experiences here, right? That exposure to his town and the people who live here will somehow magically convert you into a true believer. Is that also correct?"

Paige's eyes fell. There it was again, the thing she felt so terrible about. Any half-decent observer of human nature would recognize the early warning signs of a blossoming guilt in her downcast gaze. "Yes, you have the bet correctly stated." Even the way she phrased her admission was an indicator of her conflicted mental state. Paige watched as Mrs. Cooke processed her answer with the kind of patience that always made her uneasy. Paige knew the kind of real patience she saw in Mrs. Cooke's face often preceded real insight. She could sense what was coming before Mrs. Cooke even opened her mouth. There wouldn't be digging. Neither would Mrs. Cooke pretend Paige's gaze hadn't dropped a little too fast, or that her phrasing hadn't come pre-laminated in secret regret. Paige looked into Mrs. Cooke's eyes. She saw in them the compassion mothers have for their children. The kind of compassion which transcends all things. Heals all things. It made her so badly want to be someone's daughter. Not that Bob and Glenda didn't count as her Dad and Mom, they did. Absolutely. One hundred thousand percent. She loved them as much as she loved Jessica. It just wasn't the same. That was the thing Jessica never understood. It was how you felt when you looked in another person's eyes and saw yourself reflected in them. And not just the literal reflection of your body contained within the glassy surface of their lenses. It was about seeing the person who *made* you, looking back at you, like they would overturn everything in the world as soon as you so much as asked. She didn't remember what that feeling was like and, because of that inability to remember *them*, she didn't like Christmas.

Those two issues were intertwined in her mind. Could she tell all that to Mrs. Cooke? How would she react to the overshare? Like a mom? Or, like a person she had only known for ten minutes? Paige was in the middle of opening her mouth to find out, when Jessica catapulted through the entrance to the dining room and floated into the seat beside Paige. Having been rescued from the decision to share something personal with a stranger by Jessica's appearance, Paige followed conversational protocol by introducing Jessica to her new friend. "Mrs. Cooke, this is the co-host and producer of our podcast, Jessica Heller. Jessica, this is Mr. and Mrs. Cooke."

Mr. Cooke withdrew his scrolling finger from his phone long enough to shake Jessica's hand. "Call me

Daniel. I am nowhere near old enough to be a Mr. Cooke."

Jessica smiled politely. "Daniel it is then."

Mrs. Cooke held out her hand as soon as Jessica released her husband's. "If you're going to call him Daniel to indulge his desire not to feel old, then you simply must call me, Kelly. After all, he is five years older than I am."

Jessica shook hands with Mrs. Cooke. "It's nice to meet you, Kelly." Jessica leaned closer to Mrs. Cooke and pretended to whisper. "If you don't mind my saying, he looks at least ten years older." Mr. Cooke peered over his glasses at Jessica. He sensed it was good-natured fun and opted to participate.

"Flattery will get you everywhere, my dear."

It was in that moment Ross brought in the first trays of food laden with breakfast goodies, both sweet and salty. Eli followed with more trays. Two more trips to the kitchen by both men and the first wave, as Eli called it, was complete. He surveyed the food he had assembled for them as though it were an artistic statement. He then severed the temporary emotional connection he had made with his labor by inviting everyone to dig in. Once the plates and silverware began to clink against one another, he inquired about drink refills. Immediately upon offering, he realized Paige and Jessica hadn't even gotten their first cup of coffee, so he retreated to the kitchen to get the pot.

He filled Jessica's cup first, while saying something pleasant about the popcorn garland she had made the night before. Then he was right behind Paige. He leaned over her shoulder so he could reach the cup that was in front of her. She swore she could feel individual molecules in his outstretched arm leaping from his body onto hers. There was, at least it felt like there was, an actual physical force drawing them together. Paige wished the cup would fill with coffee before her cheeks filled with embarrassment. How was he causing this severe disorientation in her? She felt like a patient in a medically induced fog whenever he got within three feet of her body. She had to suck the electricity out of this moment, or risk pulling his mouth down to hers for a soft and precious kiss. Perplexed by his body, and lacking another option, she pretended to ignore him.

The rest of breakfast passed with Jessica and Paige trading podcast recommendations with Mrs. Cooke, while Mr. Cooke, Eli, and Ross talked about the current Patriots season and what it meant for Belichick's legacy as a football coach. Paige really didn't appreciate the gender-role sorting. She knew her idol Virginia Woolf would not approve either. Virginia taught her Shakespeare had a sister who died unknown and never wrote a word. If her feminism weren't reason enough to defy the gender sorting of the breakfast table conversation, then perhaps she could let them know she was a dyed-in-the-wool fan of the sport herself. She might cheer for the Rams, but that didn't mean she didn't have reams worth of opinions on Belichick's legacy. None of this could come out, however, because she was afraid of revealing herself to be in the opening notes of a full-blown concerto's worth of crush on her new friend Eli. For this reason, and only this reason, she traded crime show podcast suggestions with 'the girls' instead of defensive backfield rotation suggestions with 'the boys'. It took some effort, but she was able to force herself to be okay with not being a good advocate for her gender just this once.

Ian showed up when they were halfway through eating, claiming there was some project in Cabin Three he had been putting off for weeks that he wanted to work on today since it was sunny, only moderately freezing cold, and the cabin was unrented through next Friday morning. He even went as far as reminding Eli of the fact that they had spoken about the supplies for the project the day before when Eli called to ask him to wait at the bus stop for Lucy. Of course, Paige and Eli both saw through this subterfuge. Jessica, the preferred target of the ploy, played along so as to prevent any generalized table embarrassment over Ian's true intentions.

Ten minutes later, Jessica begged off going to the meeting with the mayor so that she could help Ian with the repair job he wanted to tackle. The worst part was, she acted as though she were doing it for the podcast, like it would give her a better feel for the town and how it operated at Christmas. Paige wanted to call Jessica out on her treachery but couldn't do so without making a bigger deal out of the fact that it meant she would be forced to ride into town with Eli alone than she wanted to make. Continuing in that Shakespearean vein she had begun mining in her internal monologue a few moments prior, she thought it would be a sort of 'the lady doth protest too much, methinks' kind of situation. After Jessica came up with her second, bogus, reason for indenturing herself to Ian for the day, Paige gave up arguing with her. She would just have to be strong when her body felt weak. She wasn't sure she was up to the task, but she didn't see alternatives. Hopefully, the trip would pass without him leaning over her shoulder to pour coffee in her cup.

When breakfast was complete, Eli asked Paige to

give him twenty minutes to help Ross get the cleanup underway in earnest before he would meet her in the common room. He suggested they take his SUV instead of the rental car Jessica picked up. The light snow they received during the previous night would make the four-wheel drive preferable to the all-wheel drive. Paige agreed to ride in Eli's SUV but countered with a proposal to meet on the front porch in thirty minutes rather than in the common room in twenty. She wanted to take a quick walk on the trail that wound around the lake. A few moments of communion with the beauty she found in nature here, especially while the trace snowfall hung in the trees, would do so much to wash away the loneliness of her Los Angeles life. It was one of the things she had been looking forward to ever since scrolling through the pictures of Anna's Place on the internet.

Eli readily consented, so Paige said her goodbyes to the Cookes before heading upstairs to put on her warmest clothes. Her phone was telling her the temperature outside was a ridiculous six degrees. The high for the day was forecast as twenty-three. The long-range forecast suggested today would be the warmest in Dayton until the day after Christmas. Fortunately, at least for the mayor's chances of winning his bet with Paige, she was a person who loved cold weather. She loved it even more if it came with snow. The same long-range forecast that called for extreme cold beyond Christmas, was also calling for snow to start falling early in the evening on Christmas Eve. It was not predicted to let up until late in the afternoon on Christmas Day.

Five minutes later, Paige was walking through the brisk early morning New Hampshire air bundled in her warmest cold weather gear. It was all brand new, of course. She ordered it from online sources in the weeks leading up to the trip date. Every bit of it rated at zero degrees or lower. Paige observed the clothing did its job as advertised. She didn't feel cold at all. After the first few hundred yards or so, she even unzipped her jacket to let her body breathe a little. The insulated gear would be perfect if she were jetting down a slope at Aspen, but walking at a brisk pace with no wind blowing was well below the warmth capabilities of her brand-new winter gear.

Despite the feeling she overdid the layering, Paige loved the display Mother Nature put on for her. Brilliant yellow sunshine splintered through the snow-covered trees to create a mosaic of light and dark reflections on the tranquil surface of the lake. Her breath billowed out in front of her in great clouds, as though she were a machine, or a smokestack on a miniature building. The squirrels played tag in the highest branches of the trees, doing a mesmerizing dance in slippery conditions, which was far more dangerous than their exuberant spirits seemed to realize. One false step and they would fall tens of feet to the solid frozen surface of the lake. That would be as bad as falling on concrete. Yet, no matter how much snow they scattered from the branches, they never missed their footing. They never took that plunge.

Paige carelessly, or perhaps absentmindedly, owing to the excessive beauty of the place, forgot to notice the time before she began her walk. She looked back toward the bed-and-breakfast but couldn't see it. She thought she could make out the clearing in the woods where the third cabin was but wasn't sure. Either way, her judgment of the relationship between the distance her phone indicated she traveled, and the current time, told her she had walked long enough. It was prudent she turn back so she could meet Eli on his porch.

Halfway to the house, her mind, untethered by the serenity and beauty of the lake, went rogue on her. She was seized by the idea that she should take a chance on whatever these feelings were she was having for Eli. It was as though her rational minded-self went AWOL. She wanted to be free and spontaneous. To seize the day, as the poets said. She wanted to be a version of herself which was foreign and familiar. That passionate side might be hard to find, since she had gone to impressive lengths to conceal it from the world, and from herself. But it was there. It was part of the reason she knew deep in her heart she actually...

Paige stopped the thought before it could form in her brain. She was about to complete that sentence with the words 'loved Christmas'. She couldn't allow that to happen. That was too close to something which felt like sleeping with the enemy. Sure, she could be nice to Eli. She could even think he was wildly handsome if she wanted to, but under no circumstances could she allow herself to be converted to 'loving Christmas'. It would be a complete renunciation of everything she was as a person. Her mental distance from the concept of Christmas was part of what defined her identity. Who would she be if she no longer carried that identifying mark around with her?

The front porch gradually came into view. Even from this distance, and obscured as the house was by the trees, Paige could see Eli there waiting for her. What an image it was too. He sat there in his big leather coat staring at the tiny mountains which guarded his property on both sides, like some god from Norse mythology. Paige could not deny it, or hide it any longer. She was definitely falling into a kind of emotional longing for Eli. Whatever that spark was which ignited when they first met wasn't being extinguished by spending more time in his presence. It was getting worse.

He heard her boots crunching in the snow and turned his attention to her as she approached. "How was the walk?" he asked.

Paige smiled. The absolute truth would not do in this situation. She would provide him with a highly edited version of what passed through her mind while she was communing with nature. "Wonderful. This place is so beautiful."

Eli acknowledged the truth of what she said with a nod of his head. "Of course, I can't take credit for causing the beauty, but I do appreciate it. Each and every day. It's like a palliative for the world." Eli paused and allowed his gaze to wander back over the mountains, the trees, and the fresh snow, which still had not been disturbed by gusts of wind or concentrations of sun. "Living in the city, and I don't mean to disparage your life choices at all but... living in the city, you lose track of what seeing this," Eli pointed at the beauty all around them, "does for your soul."

Paige's feelings were not hurt. "Oh, I won't take offense at that. I'm pretty sure I whole-heartedly agree with you."

Eli stood up from his rocking chair. "You ready to go?"

"As I'll ever be, I suppose," Paige replied.

Eli stepped down off the porch and drew up beside Paige as they walked toward his SUV. He would be reluctant to admit to anyone, even Ian, but he felt that same pulse-pounding sensation every time he got near Paige he used to feel when he got near Anna. He tried to paper it over with small talk. "Okay, Ms. Langford, I want you to do me a favor."

"Oh my, it sounds serious, and it must be if you're dragging out my last name." Paige responded playfully, but underneath, she was genuinely interested in what he wanted to ask her. Eli opened the passenger-side door of his SUV and held it for her while she climbed inside. "It's about Christmas."

Paige fake frowned. She could tell Eli was curious, but not in a way that would turn into a personal attack on Paige for disliking something which was of outsized importance to him and his daughter. "Uh-oh. Should I look into other accommodations while we're in town?" Paige wanted to get one more question in before she returned the conversational volley back to Eli. "And do you always hold the door open for everyone?"

Eli studied the snow-covered gravel driveway as his cheeks took on a hint of color, which wasn't caused by the sub-freezing temperatures. "No. To both questions. I'm almost at the point where I can't imagine you not being here this Christmas." That was closer to the truth about his feelings than Eli wanted Paige to be right now, so he rushed to add, "And the door-holding thing comes from my childhood. Southern boy born and raised. You gotta take the good with the bad when it comes to that. I'll let you decide if being programmed to hold the door for a beautiful woman is good or bad." Eli wondered how he had done it again. Where had that 'beautiful woman' descriptor come from? How had it jumped from his subconscious mind and gotten all entwined with the platonic intent he had for this talk? Eli reacted to try and staunch the metaphorical bleeding. The best containment solution he could think of was to shut her door. So, that was exactly what he did.

Paige, whose heart literally skipped beats for at least the fourth time since she met Eli, was not about to let him get away with that one. As soon as he opened the driver's side door enough to adequately allow her voice to pass through it, she said, "Thank you, Eli."

He considered, briefly, asking her 'for what', but decided against it. He reasoned it would take the intent behind his words from the territory of compliment and redirect them toward censure. In the end, he would have to accept the consequences of his extreme appreciation for Paige. If she chose to distance herself from the compliment, he would accept that too. It was her right as a female human person. "You're welcome," he said softly.

Paige didn't want to linger any longer over Eli's words. She sensed they were as dangerous for her as they were for him. Of course, she wasn't in a hurry to get back to the Christmas conversation either. That's what she called her continual discussions with people on the topic since her podcast aired. However, it was an easy fix for the awkwardness that was building in the cab of Eli's SUV. "So, what do you want to ask me about Christmas?"

Eli could have kissed her, both literally and figuratively, for bailing him out of his 'beautiful woman' mistake. He was eager to put as much space between him and the comment as he could. Toward the literal distance end, he started his SUV and idled down the long driveway. As the vehicle slowly approached the main road, Eli framed the first of his Christmas questions. "Okay, so stop me if I get something wrong, but as far as I was able to gather from your podcast, you have five reasons for hating, as you termed it, Christmas."

Paige nodded her head. "So far, so good."

Eli continued. "Your number one reason is," Eli paused for a moment. "Do you mind if I summarize it?"

"Like, you mean give it to me in ten words or less?" Paige smiled deeply as she thought of Jessica's critique of her. "I would love that."

Eli put his blinker on and turned onto the small highway, which would take him to downtown Dayton. "Okay, so in ten words or less, I'd say your number one reason boils down to this." Eli paused again. He was counting words in his head to see if he really could say it in ten words or less. "Why can't there be peace and goodwill all year?" Eli looked at Paige. "Am I right?"

"Perfect." Paige also started matching fingers to words. A second later she had her answer. "You did it with one word to spare too."

"Okay. Can I say something about that?" Eli asked.

"Of course." Paige braced herself for the typical counterargument she got in response to that point. Namely, a little bit of something was better than nothing of something. A form of philosophizing which prized being nice to each other once a year because it necessarily ended the possibility that we might never be nice to each other at all. To Paige, this argument was a justification for allowing yourself to be mean 364 days a year without suffering any ethical consequences. It was the least favorite response her podcast audience generated. In fact, she hated it. A part of her sincerely hoped Eli would go there. It would make it easier for her to separate from him in her mind.

"I completely agree." Eli said it with no hesitation or hint of second thoughts.

"You do?" Paige was shocked.

"I do." Eli could go her one better. "I have to deal with those thoughts every year when I trudge out to the shed to start unpacking the Christmas ornaments. It's a malaise that sets in for me sometime after I get the last dish cleaned from Thanksgiving dinner. I have that... so this is Christmas and what have you done... to make the world a better place... chorus running through my head."

Hundreds of people agreed with her statements about Christmas, but it had always been in a way that made it clear they would not be celebrating the holiday *because* of their agreement with her. Here was a man who said he agreed with her position at the same time he made his home a billowing shrine to the holiday. She had to get to the bottom of this. It caused her to sit up straighter in her seat. She was fully engaged with the conversation now. "If you feel the same way, how can you celebrate it the way you do?" Paige cast around for the first thing she could think of. "Is it because of Lucy?"

"Sure, she's part of it. It wouldn't be fair of me to keep Christmas from her because of something I felt. I mean, kids deserve to have Christmas. I think that's true." Eli covered the brake with his foot as he noticed a white-tailed deer, with fairly new antlers and not much fear of bumpers or car manufacturer's nameplates, a few hundred yards in front of them and to the right. It didn't seem to be able to make up its mind between running up the hill and jumping into the road. As they passed it, the deer chose the road, meaning Eli's anxious nature had been proved correct, again. "So, like you say, Lucy is part of it, but only the smallest part. Most of it comes from me."

Paige was struck by how interested she was in hearing what Eli had to say. Could it be she wanted to be convinced? "Lay it on me then, cowboy." Paige recoiled internally. Where had that come from? Had Eli's 'beautiful woman' comment tunneled farther into her subconscious than she thought.

"We humans are kind of sorry creatures, right? We will make this gigantic production out of peace and goodwill by having, what amounts to, a giant party one day a year to celebrate it, and then we spend the whole rest of our lives only looking out for ourselves. Honestly, we're pretty gleeful about our obsession with our own prosperity too. It's like we don't care what happens in other countries, or even other counties, as long as we have everything we need and want."

Paige couldn't resist. "Can I get an amen?"

Eli looked at her as he laughed. She was so perfect. "But..."

"I was really hoping there wouldn't be one of those." Paige hadn't been around Eli long, but she knew he wouldn't mind her playful interruptions.

"But... it's in the fact that we have a day dedicated

to peace and goodwill that I see all the future potential of our species." Eli took a minute to count the words. He gave up after losing his place the first time. "Okay, that's way more than ten words but it's pretty close to exactly how I feel."

Paige struggled mightily to hold back the tears which wanted to form in her eyes. She knew what he meant, what point he circled above. She thought it was beautiful. Still, she wanted to hear him say it, so she asked for clarification. "What do you mean by the future potential of our species?"

"Well, it seems to me the people we are when we celebrate Christmas are essentially Good People." Eli knew that didn't quite get to the heart of it, so he tried again. "It's like for a day we are all superheroes of everyday morality. If you think of the world as a fight between good and evil, or dark and light, then Christmas is a day, maybe the only day in the whole year, totally given over to harvesting light. That's what I mean when I say Christmas holds the future potential of our species. Harvesting Christmas spirit is the same thing as Harvesting Moral Light."

Paige loved what Eli had just said. He had a clear understanding of the world and the forces at work within it. It was just that the opposite side of the argument impressed her more. She pressed him for more details. "I like what you're saying. I think it is beautiful. I also think it's brazenly naïve to think we are essentially good people just because we are able to come together one day a year and not do each other extraordinary harm."

Paige weighed her phrasing and realized she might have been too harsh. "I'm sorry, Eli. I get carried away when I talk about this because it's important to me. I didn't mean to imply that your ideas were naïve. I only meant it seems to me people do a whole lot more bad than good. It seems like you are focusing on the trees to the exclusion of the forest."

Eli put on his signal to turn onto Main Street in the town of Dayton. Paige wasn't giving an inch, but neither was he. "I don't think Christmas is about the acts themselves. I think the literal good deeds people do are insignificant in the grand scheme of things. I also don't think good deeds cancel out bad deeds, or vice versa. There is no balance in the sky for all of our good and bad actions. I think it is about knowing another person. Seeing into them and letting them appreciate for this day, this hour, this moment, if that is all it can be—you care about them more than you care about yourself. To me, that is the meaning of Christmas. In the end, it's also why it doesn't bother me that the peace and goodwill don't last the whole year round. A continuous year of peace and goodwill would be amazing, but I'll take a moment of caring more about others than I care about myself if that's all I can get. I need that moment of knowing someone else is present with me in the world. It is the only valid cure for loneliness."

Because Paige didn't respond to the points in his argument, Eli pointed at the official-looking building off to their right. "That's the county office building."

Paige gave a conciliatory smile. She wanted Eli to know she enjoyed this conversation. "Saved by the bell?"

"Definitely. The question is, was it you or me?" Eli pulled into an empty parking spot and shut off the engine to his SUV.

Paige was sure it was she who had been saved.

CHAPTER SEVEN

She was very shrewd... with that extraordinary gift, that woman's gift, of making a world of her own wherever she happened to be.

Paige thought about this quote from Mrs. Dalloway as she waited on the visitor's side of the big oak desk, which belonged to Vincent Turner, mayor of the town of Dayton, New Hampshire. The clerk at the front of the building had shown her back to the office while apologizing the whole time. It seemed Mr. Turner had been delayed that morning. The words from Mrs. Woolf seemed apropos, given those circumstances.

Paige passed the time by looking over the decorations in the mayor's office to see if she could gain any insight into who he was as a person. She had long since examined the lone bookshelf in the room. It had been a dramatic letdown. Filled with books related to the history of the mayor's town, his county, and his state. Nothing that implied anything about Mr. Turner's character other than that he was a civil servant. The one thing she already knew.

As she waited, she worked back through her conversation in the car with Eli. What a morning she was having! First, she nearly jumped out of her skin when Eli leaned in close to her to fill her coffee cup at the breakfast table. Next, she was trying to enjoy a peaceful walk in nature when it spontaneously occurred to her she wanted to pursue some form of relationship with Eli, even though he lived three thousand miles away from her and was busy running a successful business while also single-handedly raising an eleven-year-old child. Finally, she came close to breaking down in front of that same man the moment he waxed poetic about his vision of humanity as symbolized by our culture's fascination with the holiday of Christmas. Paige considered herself lucky there were only a few more days until she completed her obligation and caught a flight out of this place. How much damage could she do to her knowledge of herself in a few more days?

She was solidly in the middle of contemplating the actual damage she could do when the door opened behind her. She turned to face the noise while also rising to a standing position. She held out her hand to the nice-looking middle-aged man in a bureaucrat's suit who approached her. "I'm Paige Langford," she said.

Mr. Turner extended his hand to meet Paige's. "So good to finally meet you in person, Paige. I'm Vincent Turner, mayor of Dayton. What do you think of our town so far?"

Paige couldn't answer that one with perfect truthfulness. How do you tell someone that you just met you think you may be falling in love? She opted for a blander version of the truth. "So far, it's wonderful. I really mean that."

"I knew you would love it. That's why I was willing to commit so much to this project."

The way Vincent said 'this project' caused Paige

to feel there was a lot hiding behind the words. Paige, who was already uncomfortable, immediately resolved to open the can of worms she thought the mayor's comments referenced. "About that, Mr. Turner..."

Like the Cookes before him, Vincent would not be formalized. "Please, call me Vincent."

"Okay, Vincent." Paige would not let herself be derailed by familiarity. "Let's reconsider our deal. I've come to the conclusion that it was never a good idea. I was blinded by my desire to do something I thought would be sweet for someone else, but now the whole process is just making me feel terrible." Since Vincent didn't voluntarily take his turn in the conversation when Paige left space for him to do so, Paige plowed ahead. "I mean, I've only met four people from this town in the little over twelve hours I've been here, but they were all kind, genuine people, including your clerk who works at the front desk."

Vincent refused to let any compliments of his clerk be uncorroborated. Paige thought it was a credit to his style as a boss, even if he was only an elected boss, who could be gone next year. "Oh yes, Sherrie is a true saint. People say that about other people without meaning the words in any literal kind of way. But with Sherrie, I mean it. Literally. Sometimes, I would like to nominate her for the actual title. There is no one I've met who does as much for other people as she does. She is the one who should be mayor. I tell her that every morning." His rousing endorsement of Sherrie completed; Vincent served the conversational thread back to Paige. "Sorry, I interrupted you when you were telling me why you wanted to reconsider our deal. I can get carried away whenever anyone brings up Sherrie."

Paige tried to shake off Vincent's endorsement barrage so that she remained focused on her objective, ending the deal she made with Vincent. "Yes. Please understand I have the ability to pay the town back for all the expenses Jessica and I have generated. I insist you let me do it. I don't feel I can stay here when I know it's all a hoax. Sherrie, Ian, Eli, and Lucy, there isn't one of them who deserves to be treated that way." Paige stopped for a moment. It looked to her as though Vincent was working through the things she mentioned with an open mind. She wanted to give him the chance to see she was right on his own.

"When do you do your first podcast from the bed-and-breakfast?" He asked.

"We are scheduled to do one tonight at nine o'clock. Our usual time. Just not our usual night." Paige replied.

Vincent opened a drawer on his desk and removed a plain white envelope. He set the envelope down about halfway between him and Paige. For the moment, he didn't draw further attention to it. "If you are enjoying your time here so far, why don't you just stay the course for the time being and see what happens. If, in a day or two, or when Christmas morning comes, you still feel the same way, we can talk about reimbursing the town for the expenses. Until then, let's see what develops."

Paige persisted. She was unhappy about this feeling of being dishonest with everyone she met. It was doubly important to her now that she had some citizens of Dayton who mattered more to her than they had a right to matter. "I understand your position, Vincent.

Ordinarily, I would be fine with doing something like this, but it's just Eli and Lucy are so earnest, and they seem to like me so much. I don't want to be the person who lets them down. I especially don't want to let Lucy down. I'm sure you can understand why."

"I do understand. I think the sentiment is honorable too. It shows you are a good person, and I was right to put so much trust in you when we first began negotiating our deal. For the record, you do know there is no way Lucy or Eli would find out unless you told them. I mean, you know that's true, right?" Paige intuited that Vincent was trying to put this scenario into its most basic form of black and white. He was spelling out for her that he wouldn't be the one to divulge her secret.

At last, Paige was up against it. She had nowhere else to hide. It was time to tell Vincent what her problem was with the deal, as they had agreed to it. "I don't think I can do it. I can't go on air, on my podcast, and convincingly tell my audience your town helped me find my Christmas spirit." Paige was desperate for Vincent to know she hadn't meant to do this to him. "I thought I could do it when I was in LA, but now that I'm here I know it's going to come out horrible and be see-through." Paige looked at Vincent, trying to judge if he was really hearing her. She couldn't tell either way. "People will know I'm lying."

Vincent leaned back in his chair, folding his hands loosely in front of him. Paige couldn't tell if it was calculation or fatigue. His voice, though steady, seemed to carry more weight than she expected. "Paige, you're looking at it all wrong. I don't want you to put all this pressure on yourself. I still want you to do the conversion show because it would be good for the town. At the same time, it wouldn't be in keeping with the Christmas spirit for me to ask you to give something you really don't want to give. In other words, take your time. Enjoy the next few days you have here on us. Doing that will be good for you, and it will be good for the town. I half believe we can change your mind even though you say it can't be done."

Paige interrupted him with vigor. That's how sure she was of what she was saying. "I *know* it can't be done."

"Fair enough," Vincent said. "But stay through Christmas, anyway. It would be more of a disaster for me if you left after a day than if you stayed until the end, and then went on the air and told all your listeners you actually hated Christmas more for having come here." He picked up the unmarked envelope, which lay on the table between them, and handed it to Paige. "Just do me one more favor."

Paige gave a noncommittal, "Okay."

"In the moment you are totally and absolutely sure our town has not swayed your heart, at that precise point, open this envelope and read the letter which is inside." Vincent's eyes pleaded with Paige's. He wanted her to be aware of how important her making and keeping the promise he was asking of her was to him. "I need you to do this for me more than anything else we've talked about."

Paige accepted the envelope. She slipped it into her handbag without scrutinizing it. "I can do that."

Vincent's tone turned coaxing, almost indulgent. Paige caught the shift immediately. He was trying to make her feel responsible, as though leaving would break something fragile and important. "Will you also stay? At least for another day? It would be so tragic if you left before you had the chance to see anything we do."

It felt to Paige like it was less than a half step away from emotional blackmail, but it still worked on her. "I will stay." Now that the decision was made, Paige finally relaxed a little. Interestingly, the knowledge that she would be in town for at least another day made her feel *better*. She knew it was because of Eli and Lucy. Those two had cast a deep spell on her. "I do think I should be paying my own way, though."

"Paige, if it makes you feel better, write a check for the amount this vacation would have cost and make it out to a great charity. Otherwise know that the small amount of advertising we've gotten so far from your show has already paid off. Sherrie told me this morning before you came in, she has been fielding three times the normal calls to this office looking for information about our town this week. Things like that don't happen out of the blue. We have you to thank."

"But I just..."

"It's really okay, Paige. I promise it is."

"But..."

Vincent raised a quiet hand, the kind that wasn't meant to silence but to signal a line he wouldn't keep crossing. Paige could tell that they weren't going to resolve the reimbursement debate on principle, and Vincent seemed to sense it too. Instead of continuing to argue, he opened the bottom right desk drawer and pulled out a small checkbook. The kind with white duplicate slips attached, old-fashioned and methodical.

Paige thought they were a perfect fiscal match for what she had seen of his personality so far. He flipped to a page and offered it across the desk without commentary. Paige took it and read the duplicate first, because it was the part facing her: *Anna's Place*, $1,375 signed, *Vincent Turner*. A personal check. Not town funding, not clever bookkeeping. It had always been him.

"I don't understand." Paige said.

"It might not soothe your conscience the way I'd like, but the town didn't pay for your trip here or your accommodations for the length of your stay. I did." Vincent looked at the surface of his desk for a moment because it was impossible, from where he was sitting, to get his eyes all the way to the floor. "You see, I knew you wouldn't come if you thought I was paying for everything. Involving the town made it easier for you to accept. At least, at first. The reason I had this meeting set up for right after you got here was so that I could get that cat out of the bag as quickly as possible. I knew you'd figure it out fast once you really started talking to other people from the town."

Paige could only think of one question. "But why?"

Vincent hesitated. The question lingered between them, heavier than either of them would like to admit. Paige watched him glance toward the corner of his desk. She was just about positive he was trying to avoid eye contact. Like there was something else he wasn't saying. Something that felt important enough to him to keep it tucked away until the time was right. He validated her suspicion as soon as he began talking again. "I guess I have a personal reason for wanting to see you fall in love with Christmas, but let's just say the main reason is because I love my town and I believe it can change your heart." Vincent turned his palms toward the sky as if to ask who could be responsible for the multitude of ways a fool and his money can soon be parted. "I also believe it will be money well spent regardless of the eventual outcome."

Paige thought about this new information for a minute while her eyes drifted toward the window and the snow-covered roof on the business across the street. "You know, it might be crazy, but I think it makes it better for me. It's more like an actual bet now." Paige started to get into the spirit of what Vincent was proposing. "We are like true believers of opposing viewpoints."

Paige watched something shift behind Vincent's eyes. He seemed to take stock of her reaction, the angle of her resolve softening just enough for possibility to squeeze through. "If a bet's what you need," he said, with a faint smile that didn't quite reach formality, "then let's make it a personal wager between the two of us."

Paige nodded her head. She liked this idea. "Okay. Let's do it." She held up the index finger on her right hand. "I do have one condition, though."

"Shoot."

"You let me pay you half the money back you spent on the trip. Today. I mean, like, right now. The other half we'll hold in a sort of escrow. Whoever wins on Christmas Day gets to donate it to the charity of his, or her, choice. What do you say? Do we have another deal?" Paige held out her hand.

Vincent accepted her hand in his. "If it means it will keep you here through Christmas, then deal." Vincent stood up. "Let me go get Eli and you can listen to his final plans for the Christmas Carnival on Ice."

"I can wait outside if that would be better." Paige said.

"Don't be silly," Vincent began, "you are an integral part of everything this Christmas, so I think it would be perfect if you listened in on the planning stages." With that, Vincent exited his office for the hallway which led to the lobby area.

While Paige waited, she made out a check to Vincent for half the amount she had seen on his check. She placed it underneath his office phone with most of the check protruding so he wouldn't miss it. Knowing she had now paid for half the trip relieved the greater part of the guilt she felt. As she eased back into her seat, she could hear Eli and Vincent on the way back to Vincent's office. They cluttered up the passageway with the usual forms of small talk.

That is, until Paige's ears heard something they could not quite process. It came from Eli. It sounded like he was instructing Vincent to tell Aunt Ella that Lucy wanted her to know she loved the book Ella gave her over Thanksgiving. Simple inductions led Paige to two ideas. The first was that Vincent was married to someone named Ella. The second was that Ella, and by extension Vincent, were both related to Lucy, and by extension Eli.

This was news, to say the least.

Paige saw Eli enter the room with his eyes searching for her the way eyes do when they want to find someone important to them. Her cheeks were already a little red from the Aunt Ella revelation. The fact that he wanted to find her with his eyes made those cheeks an even darker shade of red. She wouldn't allow herself to lose focus. Not now that she had a mystery to solve. All she needed was a natural break in the conversation. Or maybe not. Maybe she just had to have the answer right now. "I'm sorry." The tone of her interruption left the truth about her regret in doubt. Her dealings with Vincent were beginning to exceed Paige's tolerance for cloaks and daggers. "I mean, forgive me for eavesdropping, but are you two related?"

Eli looked at Vincent to see if he might know why this seemed to be of such importance to Paige. Vincent's face was a mask. Eli decided to field the question since Vincent's mask remained silent. "Yes, we are. By marriage. Vincent's wife, Ella, was Lucy's mother's sister." Vincent completed the relevant portion of the family tree. "Which does make me Uncle Vincent in addition to being Mayor Vincent." Vincent forced a smile. It made him look like he was in pain.

Eli could tell the news was hitting Paige far harder than it ought to. "Is something wrong, Paige?"

Paige shook her head no to indicate that she was fine. Since, in reality, she was far from fine, this took real effort. She didn't know what game Vincent was playing, but she was now sure he was playing a game of some sort. It didn't make any sense for him not to tell her he had put her and Jessica up at his brother-in-law's house. It was weird. Jessica, if she had come like she was supposed to, would say it was only a few steps removed from creepy. Despite these feelings, she managed to add words to the information she had already communicated with her nervous body language. "Nothing is wrong. Nothing at all. I just had no idea you two were related. Or maybe I was told in one of the emails and I just didn't read it closely enough."

Vincent clearly felt bad. His apology was swift. "I'm sorry, Paige. I feel like this is all my fault. I should have told you earlier. I hope you don't feel like this is a conflict of interest or something like that. I have no financial stake in Eli's bed-and-breakfast. What I am doing, I really am doing for the good of the town. Also, it doesn't hurt that there is no other place to stay within our city limits."

Paige hadn't even gotten far enough in her processing of this new development to think of it as a conflict of interest. She was still in the idea-careening phase. Since Vincent brought it up, she felt confident there was no chance it could be true, but she did make a mental note to check Google later to test the accuracy of his claim that there were no other places to stay in Dayton. "I wasn't thinking anything like that."

Paige glanced at Eli in an attempt to let him know she wasn't upset with him. Vincent had just ambushed her twice in less than fifteen minutes. That's all that was wrong with her. She found herself wishing she had Jessica here to help her steer these waters. Since Jessica was absent, she had to remove herself from the situation. That would allow Eli to finish his meeting, while also giving her space to help her think. What she needed was another hit of fresh air. "I'm going to head outside for a bit. Just walk up and down Main Street. Get a feel for the town while you two finish up. It will help me with setting the atmosphere for the podcast tonight."

Taking charge made Paige feel better. She loved solving problems. Getting out of that room was suddenly of the utmost importance to her. She was proud of herself for finding a semi-intelligent reason for accomplishing that goal. "You have my number, Eli. If you don't see me when you two are done in here, just text me. We'll find each other."

As soon as Paige said this, she got up and walked out of the office. She could tell by the silence, which reverberated in the room behind her as she made her way out, she had made an impression. She shut the door and headed down the hallway, which would take her out of the building. In the lobby area, she waved to Sherrie but didn't stop to ask her advice on where to go or what to see. She was seized with a desire to be out on the streets of Dayton by herself, under her own supervision, subject to no one's whimsy but her own. It took willpower, but she also refused her desire to call Jessica, give her the details, and ask for advice on what to do next. Paige was determined to figure this one out by herself.

She took a right as she exited the town office building and passed a restaurant whose storefront promised New York-Style Pizza. This was followed by a lawyer's office, a snappy-type car oil change place and then, personal nirvana for Paige, a used bookstore. She grasped the door handle as relief flooded her system. At last she was entering a place in this town she understood from top to bottom.

The bell chimed as she entered. It was a mechanical type alert that let Paige know the traffic counters she was used to in Los Angeles were still several years away from taking root in Roy Waller's Used Books. There was an old man behind an older register who looked like he might have lost an epic encounter with a fish while at sea several years back. Paige assumed he was the namesake Roy who graced the homemade sign which hung over the bookstore's door. She waved at him when she entered, but he had his nose in a book and didn't seem concerned about acknowledging his only customer. Paige preferred it that way.

Roy separated his 'fiction' section from his 'literature' section, so Paige skipped the Grishams in favor of the Woolfs. It wasn't that she was trying to be snobby about her reading habits. The book she was writing in that moment was an entertainment before it was anything else. She would be the first to tell you that. It was just that when she felt anxious, or worried, she liked to read something that required effort to concentrate on. It was as though the act of concentrating forced her to calm her nerves.

It was as she was handling a gently worn paperback copy of Notes from Underground by Dostoyevsky that Roy finally became aware of her. Or, at least, that was when he decided to greet her. "Let me know if you need any help," he said.

Paige thought it might have cost Roy a year or two off the end of his life to get the words out. She wondered if he hadn't spent so much time sitting in that one pose reading that his body had begun to harden, like a statue. "Thank you. I will." Paige flipped over the book in her hand. She'd read it at least four times. Why not make it five?

She carried the book to the ancient register at the rear of the store. Paige didn't see any wires going into or out of the machine. It had a hand crank on it, was made of solid oak, and would net Roy a small fortune if he put the thing up on eBay. As she set the Dostoyevsky novel on the counter, she couldn't help noticing the book he was reading. It was War and Peace. Paige smiled. "Another Russian." Roy didn't respond to her initial attempt at good-natured book small talk, so she tried another route. "I've never actually met anyone who's read that."

Roy pointed at the bookmark. It was positioned about halfway through the book. "You still haven't. I'm only on page four hundred and twelve."

Paige laughed. Roy had made a friend for life with his outstanding joke. "You must be Roy."

Roy nodded. "And you must be Paige. The city girl from Los Angeles the mayor is trying to turn into Mrs. Claus or some such nonsense."

Paige was taken aback. How had Roy known who she was? "I am her."

Roy reassured her he wasn't a psychic. "Don't look at me like I'm some kind of sorcerer. It's a small town. Far as I know, you're the only celebrity in it right now. Even if you are an internet celebrity. I guess that still counts." Roy pointed to his brain. "Two plus two, if you know what I mean."

Paige accepted the logic behind Roy's inductions. "Why is it nonsense?"

Now, Roy looked confused. "Why is what nonsense."

"What you said. About the mayor trying to turn me into Mrs. Claus." Paige offered.

"Oh, good Lord, you can't be winding that far back in a conversation with a man as old as me. That's just plain unfair."

Paige wasn't sure if Roy was making fun of himself or being serious. She pondered her responses and chose to split the difference by taking him more seriously than he probably meant for her to take him. "I'm sorry, Roy, I was just curious about exactly that fact—why is your mayor so hell-bent on turning me into Mrs. Claus. You wouldn't have any insight, would you?"

"Well, you don't get to be as old as me without learning to hold your head to the ground to see what vibrations are coursing through it." Roy chewed on his bottom lip as he closed one eye. Here was a man who knew how to strike a thinking pose. "If I had to guess, it probably had to do with Vincent's wife's younger sister Anna."

Since that matched what little bit she knew about Vincent, Paige invited more conversation on the topic. "Anna was Lucy's Mom." Paige said this to let Roy know she was aware of some of the branches on the Ryder family tree. She hoped it would make their conversation easier.

"Oh yeah, and if you know Lucy, then you know Anna was quite a person. She was like a giant magnet in the center of every room she entered. Some people are stars and some people are planets. Anna was definitely a star—you remind me a lot of her, actually. Even though I've only been knowing you these past five minutes. You have that same star-like quality about you."

Paige smiled bashfully, the way anyone would when receiving a wonderful compliment like that. "Thank you, Roy, but I'm sure I'm much closer to an asteroid than a star." Paige paused to reengage with the previous thread of conversation. The one where she was learning something about the mysterious reasons why Vincent wanted to convert her into a true believer so badly. "Is there anything you can think of that might explain the mayor's strange behavior? Anything at all would be really helpful to me. I'm at a loss right now."

Roy thought about it for several more moments. His eyes developed that squinty look that signals when a person is trying hard to find something in their memory. Paige recognized those signs and refrained from saying anything that might derail the train of associations going on in his mind. All at once, his face brightened. Obviously, a light bulb had gone off.

"What is it?" Paige asked breathlessly. She was doing a poor job of maintaining an aura of detachment from her desire to know whatever it was Roy remembered.

"Oh my! I do have something for you. I'll be right back." Roy disappeared into the back, Management Only, area of his store. He returned to the register counter a couple of minutes later carrying one of those plastic gray boxes college and high school students used to fill with index cards back in the eighties and nineties. Paige thought the organizational system was true to form for an old codger who refused to adopt the ultra-modern ways of the Information Age. Who else, she thought, would still find satisfaction in running a used bookstore than someone who stored important things in gray plastic index card boxes? Roy opened the one he was carrying to reveal the three by five cards Paige expected. He flipped through them until he found the card which caused his search in the first place. He pulled it out and handed it to Paige.

Paige quickly absorbed the information on the card. There were at least a dozen entries, but four of them particularly stood out to her. They were her four novels for young adult readers. The dates beside them were all from that year's summer season. "I don't understand," Paige said.

Roy loved that he had a captive audience. That's why he dragged out his delivery. "Flip the card over."

Paige did as she was told. There were two words directly in the center of the card. They were all in capital letters and were written by a hand with a refined cursive script. That hand had been at the activity of labeling index cards for so many years it had perfected the activity. The words were:

LUCY RYDER

Paige's jaw dropped. She finally connected the dots. "Are these dates on here when she came in and bought these books."

"Yes, that's why it took me so long to put it all together. She bought the first one back in the spring. That's on the outer edge of how far back I go out of my way to try and keep my customer's buying patterns in my mental files. I've been using these index cards to keep track of what they like, so I don't have to do it myself, ever since I sold my first few books. In this case, my system almost let me forget the most important part of the story.

The fact Lucy is an avid fan of *your* novels for young adults."

"Do you think that might be part of the reason Vincent invited me here?" If Roy did think that, Paige never got to find out. In just that moment, the front doorbell chimed as someone opened it. Paige turned to look. Eli stood in the bright sunlight looking like something out of an old cowboy movie. The sun and the snow were conspiring to black out his features as he stood in the doorway. He was probably standing there so long because his eyes needed to adjust to the much dimmer conditions within the store.

"Hey stranger," Paige volunteered. She didn't want Eli to think she was snooping on his family, so she quickly pulled a five-dollar bill from her purse. She used the cash because she didn't want to take the time to find out if Roy accepted debit cards. She was aiming to make it seem to Eli as though all she had been doing in this store was looking for a good book to read. "Thank you so much for the conversation, Roy. I'll keep your recommendations in mind. I'll also take this book if you don't mind parting with it." Paige was sure she was making a first-order spectacle of herself by going to such lengths to seem as though nothing out of the ordinary were happening. Roy took so long working his ancient register, Paige was also sure Eli would reach her before the transaction completed. Eli was now only five feet away, and that card was lying on the counter directly beside her Dostoyevsky book. It was face up so that the words 'LUCY RYDER' were clearly visible. Paige thought it would be a disaster if Eli saw that card sitting next to the book she was buying.

Roy continued to manipulate the levers and gears

on his register with such ferocious lack of competence, Paige was convinced he actively conspired with Eli to let him see the index card with his daughter's name on it. There wasn't any other explanation for his maddening behavior. At the very last moment, she did the only thing she could think of. She grabbed the Dostoyevsky book from the counter and used her thumb and index finger to pick up the card in the process. She had no idea how smoothly the operation went, but she did take possession of the card before Eli had a chance to read it. At least, she hoped she had. The convergence of his arrival at the service counter, with her scoop maneuver performed on the card, was nearly perfect.

"Imagine that. I found the author at the bookstore." Eli smiled as he delivered his greeting to Paige. "How are you doing today, Roy?"

"Just fine, how about yourself?" Roy asked.

"Can't complain." Eli answered.

"But sometimes you still do." Roy replied.

Paige recognized the grooves of familiarity these two had in their conversation as confirmation of Lucy's statement from yesterday evening about the Ryder's weekly trips to the bookstore. "How many places did you try before you found me?" Paige asked Eli.

"This was the first." Eli fixed Paige with a look she thought overflowed with ambiguous aplomb. "Did you find what you were looking for?"

The double entendre floored Paige. Was it meant or unmeant? She did not expect to be called out on her fact-finding mission. She tried to keep her tone from sounding defensive as she responded, "I'm not sure I know what you mean."

Eli looked at her as though she were being stubborn, or intentionally dense. He pointed to the book in her hand. "The book. Did you find something you want to read? I should have told you I have an extensive library at the house. I include that in the tour I give. I noticed Lucy forgot to point it out when she showed you around yesterday. I think she got too caught up in showing you her own room." Eli couldn't grasp why Paige looked embarrassed. He decided to wrap up his personal collection offer. "You could have looked there before coming here." Eli paused because Paige's facial expressions just weren't meeting him halfway. He redirected the conversation a third time to try and give himself a harbor. "What did you get?" he asked.

"Notes from Underground."

"Oh, that's a classic. I love that one. Most people go with Crime and Punishment or The Brothers Karamazov, but I'll take Notes every day of the week. Of course, cases can be made for The Idiot and The Possessed as well." Eli's face took on the expression of someone who has thought of something important. "Old translations or new?"

They both said, "Old," at the same time. Paige laughed. She couldn't remember the last time she had talked with someone who could rank her favorite books, by one of her favorite authors, in the exact order she would rank them. The fact that he also preferred the older translations was icing. Paige turned her attention back to Roy. "Thank you again, Roy. I'm sure I'll come back and see you again before I leave." When she did come back, she would also thank him for not blowing her cover with Eli. Right after she gave him his card on Lucy's buying habits back.

"Please do. And as long as we're talking about great Dostoyevsky novels, don't forget Poor Folk. Just because it was his first, that doesn't mean it was his worst." Roy waved his hand at the rows of books that lined his store. "I even have a copy in there somewhere."

"Put it on hold for me then. I promise I'll come get it before Christmas Eve." Paige gave Roy a small hug, an act which made his entire month, before hitting Eli with, "You ready to go?"

"Well, as my grandfather used to say," Eli held the moment for a beat just to lend it a sense of quasi-dramatic urgency, "if you're waiting on me, you're backing up." Paige looked at Eli without endorsing his grandfather's saying. "Yeah, I didn't much get it either." Paige still showed no signs of approval. "I think maybe it came from a song." Less than nothing from Paige. "Anyway, it was good seeing you, Roy. Lucy and I will make it around just after Christmas. Or maybe we'll come whenever Paige comes."

"I look forward to seeing all three of you," Roy said with sincerity.

Paige felt her stomach drop at the mention of Lucy in connection with Roy's bookstore. She found herself wishing she had a few more minutes with Roy. She might have been better able to decipher what was going on in this sleepy town and why she was so essential to its Christmas. She just knew if she had been allowed five more minutes with the old-timer, she would have learned something important. Still, the information she got from him was a start. It would be up to her to distill it for its truth.

Part of her relished the challenge.

CHAPTER EIGHT

Not for weeks had they laughed like this together, poking fun privately like married people.

This quote from Mrs. Dalloway ran through Paige's mind as she and Eli walked out into the brilliant sunlight reflecting off the previous night's snow. She blinked her eyes furiously as her pupils adjusted to the rapid change in brightness from the interior of Roy's used bookstore. She also fought back, hard, against the impulse which consumed her. She wanted to take Eli's hand in hers. It was official. It had become a theme. Every time she spent more than thirty seconds with Eli, her mind devolved into some sort of emotional hypoxia. The result of this condition was that her body wanted to be nearer to his body. She wondered how many more of these mental faintings she could endure before she did something completely off the wall like, God forbid, pull his mouth to hers. The warmth that coursed through her as she had this thought had nothing to do with the Arctic sun, which was shining on her. She needed a change of subject, fast. Before more of Virginia Woolf's sentences about laughing and married people roared through her head and fanned her desire.

"Okay, so this morning you got me pretty good with your 'future potential of the species' argument in favor of Christmas. That is, I must admit, the first time anyone has ever provided a coherent counterexample to my point about spreading peace and goodwill year-round rather than just at Christmas." This was Paige's way of letting Eli know that he had impressed her with his critical thinking abilities.

"I sense there is a monumental 'but' coming." Eli smiled brightly as he said this. He was getting more enjoyment out of upsetting Paige's anti-Christmas apologetics than he was in preparing for the actual holiday itself.

"But that was only the first premise in my discussion. What do you make of point number two?" Paige asked.

"That Christmas is basically a consumerist feeding frenzy?" Eli counted the words in keeping with their new habit when discussing this subject. "Only eight words, nice! Once again we are under the ten-word maximum."

Paige laughed at their small inside joke. "Nice job." While giving herself time for her gentle peals of laughter to settle, Paige tried to think of the perfect way to frame her position. She had sharpened these spears many times before with others on the internet, but Eli was in a class by himself. She wanted to make sure the spears she launched in his direction were precisely sharpened. "I mean, it feels like the true spirit of the holiday has been overrun by the ceaseless march to commodify everything that has ever been associated with the idea of Christmas. Name something even in the same ballpark as Christmas and I can find you ten places to buy it online in less than ten seconds."

"I don't suppose it will count as a defense if I point out our culture has commodified everything, will it?" Eli knew it wouldn't count. He just wanted to make sure he and Paige were being clear about the starting points of their discussion.

"Of course not. If Christmas is to be an expression of our 'future potential as a species', then it cannot be wrapped in the gauzy-slick paper of the present." Paige was proud of herself. She thought that was the most eloquent she had ever been on the subject.

"Fair enough." Eli had no problem granting Paige made a great point.

Paige erupted with spirit. "Does that mean you submit? Are you willing to admit I am right about that part of Christmas?"

"I didn't say that." Eli watched as Paige frowned. He could tell she wanted to get the best of him on this one. However, he wasn't prepared to vacate the field that quickly. He had a response or two tucked up his sleeve. "You make a strong point; I'll give you that. But I don't think you are examining the act of buying in the proper isolation. Generally speaking, Christmas is the only time of year when large swaths of people give gifts without expecting the 'credit' to accrue to them for having given the gifts."

Paige saw where he was going with this. It troubled her. Once again, he was delivering an argument she wasn't prepared for. "You're talking about Santa, aren't you?"

"Yep." Eli's grin overspread his face. Paige could tell he felt he had her on the intellectual ropes of her own prize-fighting ring.

Paige sighed. There was probably no way she could salvage this round either. "Okay, let me have it."

"The way I see it, most of the time when you, and by you I mean anyone, not you specifically, give a gift to another person you want them to know it was from you almost more than you want them to really like it."

"You want the 'credit'." Paige finished the thought for Eli.

"Exactly. You want them to see you know them so well you picked out the perfect gift for who they are as a person. Or, you want them to know you spent X amount of dollars on them, where X is some exorbitant number that is more than you could, or should, actually afford." Eli saw in Paige's face that she agreed with what he was about to say. "And yet, every year millions of gifts are given in which no person is attributed as the buyer. It ranges from the kids who are young enough to believe in the Christmas magic of an actual Santa Claus, all the way up to the secret Santa traditions which have become widespread in the modern workspace."

Paige's brain slowly conformed to the quality of Eli's ideas, which were taking shape within it. "Okay. Your point about present attribution isn't bad. However, that doesn't lessen the hypocrisy in the story you hear at least once every Black Friday about two people punching one another to get the last one-hundred-and-fifty-inch flat screen TV on sale for twenty-three dollars."

Eli laughed out loud. He couldn't help it. Paige's exaggerations were so over the top. "One hundred and fifty inches?"

"Actual size may vary."

"And twenty-three dollars?"

Paige would not be driven from the main idea. "You know what I mean. And you hear it every year. We have become immune to the stories, but they still happen. I remember the first time I heard it. It was about a worker in one of the big chain stores who got trampled. That was all the way back when I was a freshman in college." Paige's face showed how important this was to her. She wanted Eli to know she wasn't just bringing up someone being trampled in order to score points in a silly argument over the merits of Christmas. She wasn't crass. Incidents like that made headlines, and people talked about them around the watercooler for a few days, but then most people forgot. Paige never forgot.

Eli nodded his head. He also remembered the tragedy she alluded to. "Thankfully, retailers have begun taking their worker's safety more seriously since that happened." Eli paused—thinking, maybe reconsidering. But the way his brow stayed smooth, and his voice stayed firm, told Paige her argument hadn't swayed him. "I can tell it's important to you that Christmas be removed from its pedestal. And I won't even argue with you when you make most of your case. I think we have gotten away from a lot of the principles that make Christmas worthwhile in favor of shortcuts which make it easier for us to celebrate. As with everything else in our modern life, we trade value for appearance. The younger generation takes it to extremes with their reliance on social media to validate an event actually happened. But I think Christmas is special. I think it is full of real emotions. I think the reason it persists from generation to generation is because it is built on a great idea." Eli let that last bit simmer before completing his monologue with an appropriate Christmas thesis. "Forget yourself for a day." Eli again counted the words. "Hey, I did it in five that time. I'm getting better."

Paige stopped in front of the passenger's side door of Eli's SUV. Their conversation had brought them all the way back to the vehicle which would carry them home. She looked at him with something approaching love building in her eyes. "You are impossible." Suddenly overcome by the spontaneous sort of emotion Wordsworth would have encapsulated in a poem about clouds and flowers, Paige thrust herself onto her tippy toes and kissed Eli on the cheek. Her action took the breath away from both of them. It was several skipped heartbeats later before either of them was able to speak.

"What was that for?" he asked in a whisper.

"For being you." Paige responded.

"Will you do it again, if I promise to keep being me?" Eli wondered, as a sly grin spread across his face.

Paige rippled with laughter. She hadn't meant to kiss him, even if it were hardly more than a peck. Still, he handled her trespass against the boundaries of friendship with great dignity. If she were to judge by the fact that he hadn't tried to escape her body when she pressed it against his, or the fact he asked her to do it again, she would wager he enjoyed the physical contact with her. "We'll see. I can tell you it isn't likely to hurt if you keep being you."

Eli opened the door of his SUV for her and then stepped around it to let her enter. Eli looked up at the cloudless sky—silent and bright. Paige couldn't tell what he was searching for, but something about the way he lingered made her wonder what question he'd just asked the sky without saying it out loud. "In that case, I promise to keep being me for as long as it takes."

As Eli shut the door, Paige wondered why she was letting her feelings get the best of her. She didn't need to be doing this. Four million people lived in Los Angeles. Roughly two million of those people had to be men. The odds were, of those two million men, at least one was as good-looking and as fundamentally genuine as Eli. There simply had to be someone in her own city who would match the qualities she was looking for in a man. Except she hadn't been looking. That was what made Eli such a revelation. He appeared when she wasn't looking for commitments or entanglements at all. She was smack in the middle of taking Peter's classic advice of going 'straight on till morning' when the force of him ambushed her tranquility.

She watched as he circled his vehicle. She tried to place what it was that caused these feelings in her. Of course, she had been affected from the beginning by his tremendous physical beauty—but that kind of thing happened often enough she couldn't attach any special significance to it in Eli's case. And yet, from the moment she first saw him, she had been drawn to him in a way she couldn't fully explain within the normal rules of attraction. Her need to be around him had a definitive 'at first sight' quality to it. The kind of thing that couldn't be tamed. The kind of thing that grew and grew, in the same way scientists said black holes grew and grew. Was that what was going on? Had Eli Ryder become a giant black hole in the center of the Paige Langford galaxy?

She didn't have more time to devote to the issue because Eli entered his SUV and began to question her as soon as he slid into the driver's seat, while simultaneously hitting the key to start the vehicle. "So, now we've been through two of your five points," Eli began, "and I am sure that, so far, the advantage belongs to me." Eli dropped the transmission into reverse while checking the backup camera to be sure his route was clear of obstacles.

"Slight advantage." Paige had to claim some ground in this Christmas contest or Eli would smell blood in the water. The rout would be swift.

"Fair enough. I'll take that. So far, I have a *slight* advantage." Eli shifted into drive and eased the SUV onto the small highway, which would take them back to his home. "Shall we move on to point three?"

"We shall," Paige agreed.

"If I remember correctly, point three was that it gets earlier every year." Eli looked at Paige to see if he had stated her thesis in a way she found acceptable.

Paige gave him visual confirmation that she agreed with his restatement. She then added, "You hit the nail right on the head," just to be sure there was no ambiguity.

"Okay. Well..." Eli stuttered for a moment. This was far more for effect than from any real loss of words. "I'm kidding. I don't have anything to say to that. It does get earlier every year. I swear I walked into Walmart this year in September for a new bathing suit, and they were setting up their Christmas department."

Paige was so happy Eli had granted her the point. She reacted by calling out what was, to her, the most blatant abuse of this failure to observe any Christmas downtime during the regular part of the year. "The Hallmark Channel even started airing Christmas movies all year round this past year." Paige held her hands up as though this was the most outrageous of crimes. "I mean, how can it be special if it never stops?"

"I hadn't heard that, but I totally agree. Christmas spirit is free to travel throughout the calendar, but the commodification of Christmas should be limited to the month of December." Eli allowed Paige room to add to his comments. Since it marked the first time they had been in complete agreement on this subject, which was important to both of them, if for wildly different reasons, he wanted to make sure she had her say too.

On her side of the SUV, Paige felt like calling an end to all this Christmas discussion by giving him another kiss. The fact that he was willing to be truthful even if it contradicted his ideas, that was a thing worth immortalizing in a person. Most everyone she knew would rather be hobgoblins to their foolish consistencies than admit real arguments came with nuance. Paige thought if she lived in New Hampshire, or if Eli and Lucy lived in Los Angeles, they would have a serious future as a family unit. Unfortunately, neither of those things was true, or had any possibility of becoming true. Paige didn't want to think about that right now, so she used the conversational space Eli allotted her to move the discussion forward. "So, we agree to disagree on points one and two." Paige inclined her head toward Eli slightly, "while acknowledging you did a better job of supporting the ProChristmas position than I did of supporting the AntiChristmas position."

"Thank you. Thank you very much." Eli said this in an Elvisy way that was meant to exercise the tiniest bit of grandstanding.

"And we both agree that I have carried the day with point three." Paige adopted Eli's grandstanding tones for the celebration of her victory. A case where the enjoyment she took in Eli's mind spilled over into a reflective speech pattern any decent psychologist would recognize as one of the first signs of a deepening crush. "Which means, if we are keeping score..."

"Because everyone knows Christmas is about winning." Eli's brief sideways glance told Paige he wasn't criticizing her. Although Christmas was important to him, he would always be the type who could also laugh at the things he wanted to take seriously.

"Everyone knows that," Paige agreed with a smile.

"Then the score is two to one in favor of the gentleman from New Hampshire." Eli summarized.

"Fortunately for me, we are in a best of five series." Paige mentally flipped through the two remaining points in her AntiChristmas dissertation. "Do you think it would be okay if I choose which one of the remaining points we tackle first?"

Eli had no problem with this. "By all means," he said.

Paige exhaled relief. "In that case, I'm going to skip ahead to number five. I feel I'm on much safer ground there. At least in terms of being right. Although I get more emails calling me out for being a Grinch, or much, much worse, being a you-know-what that almost rhymes with Grinch, on this one than the other four combined."

"Man, I knew the moment you asked for home-court advantage I was in serious trouble." Eli looked like he was conceding. "Can I change my mind and insist we go in order? I'm much more confident I can show Christmas is NOT useless to those without a family."

"Oh no, way you agreed! You don't think you can win point five, do you?" Paige was happy. She was already moving her mental scoreboard to a four-game tie. It looked to her like they would be headed toward a decisive fifth and final match.

Eli sighed. "I admit it's very hard to defend the practice of continuing the Christmas Tree—in either of its instantiations." He quit talking to let her win her point in her own words.

Paige gleefully jumped in. "Obviously, it doesn't make much sense to cut a tree down for one month of use and then discard it as though its entire purpose in the universe had been to sit in a red metal stand surrounded by big boxes wrapped in brightly colored paper and bows."

"Agreed."

"And the plastic trees are worse. I mean, it is true they can be used for several years. But how long is several years, really? Ten? Maybe fifteen years? At the most. And then what? It's going to be thrown away. Seriously, I researched this, and although I couldn't find anyone willing to toss out an actual number, the words most commonly used were 'vast majority'. As in the 'vast majority' of fake trees end up in a landfill." Paige stopped out of courtesy to Eli. She knew how she was when she got going. She might start monologuing, and she didn't want to do that. She wanted this to be a discussion. She had so much respect for Eli she needed for it to remain a discussion.

Eli ran his left hand across his jaw. Paige wondered if it was a subconscious habit he had when he was thinking hard. Was she making him think hard? "Those are both good points. I admit."

"Do you yield?" Paige's smile let Eli know her hyper-competitive language was all in good fun.

"Not yet. I do have a few things that need to be said in defense of the trees. I may not carry the day, but I've cut down too many of them not to say anything."

"Fair enough," Paige said.

"Okay, so the first point is that the tree is a tradition which goes back hundreds of years."

Even though Paige sensed what Eli was going to do with this premise, her growing appreciation of his mind allowed her to willingly walk into a potential trap. She had ammunition. She hoped it would land. "Lots of things are well-regarded traditions in one century which are shown to be absolute barbarity in the next. History is riddled with these traditions. In fact, every culture that survives more than a few hundred years is riddled with them." Paige had this line prepared beforehand. She had met this 'tradition' argument too many times in the emails to her blog not to have a steady answer memorized for whenever it got deployed.

"I'll grant what you say is true in a general way, but

I don't think it applies to the specific case of Christmas Trees." Eli slowed down and put on his left-hand turn signal. The long driveway to his house was approaching. "I think you are making an argument by analogy, and as I'm sure you know, those arguments, while persuasive, are never valid."

Paige was struck to the center of her heart, again. She knew her anti-tradition argument wasn't valid, but no one else in the world had called her out on it before. Eli was ridiculously handsome, a warmly sympathetic father to his eleven-year-old daughter, and one of the smartest people she had met in the last ten years. That was a combination of factors one didn't often find in a person. It was a combination of factors that suggested to Paige there was some possibility she had found *the one for her*.

Paige sensed Eli was parsing her silence for its meaning and coming up empty. "Does that mean you agree with me?"

"You're right about the argument by analogy, but not about the trees." Paige hoped he would say something else that would keep her from thinking he was the one for her again.

Eli smiled as he pulled into his parking spot in front of the bed-and-breakfast. "You know how many trees I've got inside that house, right?"

Paige returned his smile as she counted the trees she had seen in his house. "Is it ten?"

"Not quite, but close." His eyes asked for forgiveness. "Don't hate me. I really like Christmas trees."

"Liking something doesn't count as a premise in an

argument either. If I can't have my analogy, you can't have your likes." Paige wouldn't yield. This was too important to her.

"I like you. Does that count for anything?"

The moments spilled past her as Paige tried to think of something witty to say in response to Eli's mini-confession. Was this how it went when two people who were supposed to be together forever finally met? She saw a certain narrative necessity to it. If there were just one person for her, and if that person was Eli, then everything she had been feeling since she met him at the airport the day before made sense. It would be part of the story they told their grandchildren... at Christmas. Oh Lord, she saw it in isolation now. She wasn't only falling for Eli...

She was falling for Christmas too.

That *could not* happen. She was not some throwaway Hallmark heroine.

"Thank you for letting me ride with you to see the mayor." Paige's voice betrayed the uncertainty in her heart.

Eli noticed. He wanted the Paige from two minutes ago back. "What's wrong?" he asked.

"Nothing," Paige lied. She hopped out of Eli's vehicle and shut the door behind her.

Eli had no idea what he had done wrong.

CHAPTER NINE

It is a thousand pities never to say what one feels...

The feelings which coursed through Paige after her dual realization about Eli and Christmas overwhelmed her. She made a beeline for the house and the safety of her upstairs room. She knew this must have confused Eli. He didn't deserve to be treated that way. At the same time, she had no intention of letting him see her cry. Since crying had been exactly what she would have done, if she had continued her discussion with Eli in the wake of the knowledge that she was beginning to fall for Christmas as well as him. So, she beelined it for her room instead. And Virginia was right again. It is a thousand pities never to say what one feels.

Once there, she sorted herself by focusing on the more mundane activities of her writer's life. She opened her laptop and went through those ever-present emails. She even thought about cracking the figurative spine of the new novel she was writing. Ultimately, she chose not to do that because her present mood didn't match the tone of the chapter she was working on. She had never been one of those authors who could work on a story out of sequence, so she accepted she wasn't going to get any novel writing done that afternoon.

She ended by drafting an email to her agent, letting

her know she didn't appreciate the continual pressure to sell the rights to the podcast. Paige insinuated her level of dislike was so great she was thinking of looking for a new agent to represent her. Perhaps she could find one who wouldn't be so adamant about not following her client's wishes. She only drafted, rather than drafted and sent, the email, because she lived by the standard that you never send written correspondence when you are upset. It was just true that you had no idea how it would sound to you later when you weren't upset. She was about to close the laptop and move on to the novel despite her mood, when a new email arrived in her inbox. The sender's name piqued Paige's interest, so she immediately opened it.

Mrs. Cooke had found her on the internet. In the hours since breakfast, Mrs. Cooke's email informed Paige, she had listened to several of her podcasts and downloaded one of her eBooks. She had done all this while Mr. Cooke continued to read stories on his phone about his beloved New England Patriots. An observation which inspired Mrs. Cooke to wonder why she ever quit her job. Surely, she mused, this was not what people were referring to when they talked about enjoying the last years of their lives in the luxury of retirement. Her email went on to inform Paige she had also listened to the Anti-Christmas podcast, which had been the cause of Paige's trip to New Hampshire. She ended by telling Paige she was available to talk at any time.

Paige reached the end of the message and hit the little arrow button to craft a reply. She was ten words into her answer when she thought better of it. An email response wasn't what was required. Mrs. Cooke said she was 'available to talk at any time'. She meant those last three words so much she had put them in italics to give them extra emphasis. Paige thought she might see if those were empty words on Mrs. Cooke's part, or if she meant what she wrote, literally. She would go see Mrs. Cooke. She would go see her right then and there.

Paige shut the laptop. She stood and grabbed her coat from the bed where she had set it when she had entered the room twenty minutes before. It would be a little awkward if she saw Eli this soon, given the way she ran off on him after they got back from town. But that was a risk she was willing to take. Her desire to talk to Mrs. Cooke festered within her. What Paige really needed and wanted in this moment was the one thing she never had access to, a mother to listen to her, or a father to hug her and tell her everything was going to be okay, whether it was true or not.

Paige needed a family.

She didn't want this to imply she didn't love her adoptive parents. Her love for them was limitless. They had done more for her than she could ever repay, no matter how long she lived. The source of this family wish of Paige's wasn't related to a defect in Bob and Glenda's parenting. Instead, it traced back to the desire she had felt since the night of the accident to be in her biological parents' presence one last time. It was about the way her mother's hands used to curl her hair into braids on Sunday mornings before they went to church. The way she would sing her lullabies on the nights she put Paige to bed. It was about the way her father would read to her from big books on the nights he put her to bed. How she would always ask for one more chapter. How he would always read it. No matter how tired they both knew she was. These were the things she missed. These were the things she wanted back. She knew how beautiful Bob and Glenda's love for her had been. But they couldn't provide everything she needed because she had known her parents. She remembered her parents. Her parents were beautiful people too. Bob and Glenda, despite their best efforts, could never erase the fact that she missed her parents.

Paige eased out of her bedroom. As silently as possible, she latched the door. She thought about checking for Jessica to see if she had returned, but the extreme quiet which emanated from Jessica's room told her she was still off somewhere. If she knew Jessica the way she thought she did, then whatever she was doing would be certain to involve falling more deeply in love with Ian. Paige wondered what got into them on the plane ride here that made them so vulnerable to their romantic natures. Neither of them thought of themselves as subject to the societal construct which required all women over a certain age find someone to spend their time with. How it happened they both struggled with the most naïve of all romantic notions, the idea of love at first sight, at the same time, was beyond Paige's ability to reconcile. If she could ever corner Jessica for five consecutive minutes, she would probably ask her for her input.

Paige slipped down the stairs, through the main hallway, and all the way to the front door without arousing detection. Her heart beat in her chest like a freight train by the time she opened the screen door and set foot on the front steps. If she had run into Eli while he gathered wood from the stack on the extreme left corner of his porch, she would have screamed.

Paige couldn't have known it, but she had no reason to worry on that count. As fate, or luck, would have it, Eli was down at the bus stop waiting for Lucy. Today was the last day before Christmas break. This meant Lucy's school dismissed three hours early. It was now just after noon and the bus wouldn't arrive for another twenty minutes, but Eli was already at the bottom of the driveway with his nose in a book. Paige would have been pleased to know that it was one of her books. She would be further pleased to know that, although his eyes scanned the words on the pages, his mind was preoccupied with sorting through the details of his morning conversation with her. He remembered the parts that were beautiful to him while also examining the ending to try and determine how their talk went off the tracks.

Paige hurried down the steps and took the trail that led to Cabin One. It was only a few hundred yards until she reached the front door, yet it felt to Paige like every step was part of some grueling 5k race held on the side of a mountain. She felt exposed. She didn't want Eli to see her. She didn't want Jessica to see her either. It wasn't in Paige's nature to ask for help, but that's exactly what she was doing by going to see Mrs. Cooke. The fact Mrs. Cooke didn't even know she was coming made it worse.

Paige knocked twice and then regretted coming. She was in the middle of contemplating running away, all the way back to Los Angeles kind of running away, when Mr. Cooke opened the front door of Cabin One. "Can I help you?" he asked with a bewildered tone.

"Would I be able to speak with Mrs. Cooke for a

moment?" Paige braced herself for the worst. She tried to puzzle out what she would do if Mr. Cooke told her his wife had left the cabin for the day. Maybe she went to get her hair done or visit a sister in a nearby town. All of these thoughts traipsed through her brain in the microseconds before Mr. Cooke invited her into the tiny living room area of the quaint little cabin. An obvious sign to Paige's fevered mind that Mrs. Cooke was somewhere in the belly of the cabin after all.

"Come on in and have a seat on the couch." Mr. Cooke stepped to the side so she could perform the activity he suggested for her. He then shut the door behind her. "Kelly was taking a dip in the jacuzzi." Mr. Cooke put a conspiratorial hand up to his mouth and then added to the effect by talking out of the side of his mouth. "I can hardly get her out of that thing the whole time we're here." After delivering this comment, replete with the odd hand gesture, he went back to his usual mode of speaking. "I'll run to the bedroom and let her know you've dropped by, and you want to speak with her."

Paige had been feeling worse and worse from the moment she stepped into the Cooke's cabin. She had made a mistake in coming, and that mistake grew more pronounced by the second. Her presence in their afternoon would end up putting these good people out. Who was she to intrude on their ability to enjoy a quiet vacation together as a couple? Mrs. Cooke didn't have time for Paige. It should have been sufficient for Paige that she had been nice enough to take a look at her podcasts and download one of her books. How could Paige justify coming here and interrupting Mrs. Cooke's time with her jacuzzi? She couldn't. Mr. Cooke was almost in the tiny hallway, which led to the back bedroom. If she didn't stop him right away, it would be too late. Paige couldn't let that happen. There had to be a way to undo what she had done by knocking on the door of Cabin One. "Mr. Cooke..."

Mr. Cooke interrupted, "Please, Paige. Call me, Daniel."

Paige lined up her courage to try again. "Daniel. I should not have come over unannounced like this. I'll just leave and see if I can meet up with your wife at dinner."

As Paige completed her sentence, Mrs. Cooke entered the living room. "Nonsense," she said. "I'm here now, and I am very curious about what you have to say." She directed a disinterested shooing motion at her husband. "You should go on back and get in the jacuzzi while it's still warm. It'll do wonders for your arthritis."

Mr. Cooke frowned at his wife. Paige got the feeling they had been having this same pretend fight for decades. "You know how much I hate those things. I haven't taken a bath in fifty years. I have no idea why you think I'd like to take one just because we're on vacation."

"It's not a bath, it's a relaxation machine. You'd think with all the pain you're always talking about you'd be agreeable to a solution, even if it were only temporary." Mrs. Cooke intended all this for Mr. Cooke's own good, but you'd never know it from the look on his face.

"I'm going to go take a shower, because that's what I do. I take showers. It's what I've done for the past fifty years. It's what I'll do for however many years I have left on this planet." Mr. Cooke pointed to the wedding band on his left hand. "How long have we been married, Kelly?"

"Too long if you ask me." Mrs. Cooke didn't mean

it. Mr. Cooke knew it. They were just enacting their parts in the grumpy old married couple play they put on for company. It gave them pleasure to ruffle each other's feathers, since both knew neither one meant any of it seriously. It was a side benefit that whatever company they found themselves in was inevitably entertained by their antics. The fact was, they did it to entertain themselves.

"Twenty-five years!" Mr. Cooke continued as if his wife hadn't insulted their marriage. "And in those twenty-five years, how many baths have I taken?"

"I am not the official record-keeper for the number of baths you've taken." Mrs. Cooke said most of this to his back as he left the room.

Mr. Cooke knew the longer he stayed in her presence, the more likely it was she would become insistent about his need to get in the jacuzzi. His best bet was to escape while he could with his fifty plus year streak of not taking a bath still intact. "Zero," he said from the relative safety of the bathroom. Paige could hear water beginning to fall in the shower. "You don't need to be a record-keeper to remember something that has happened zero times, Kelly." Attempting to make sure he would get the last word, Mr. Cooke shut the door to the bathroom.

Mrs. Cooke looked at Paige. "Sorry about that, dear. And don't let my grizzled tone fool you. I worship the ground that arthritic old stick in the mud walks on. I just can't let him know it." Mrs. Cooke winked at Paige. "Now, to what do I owe the pleasure of your early afternoon visit?"

The words collected at the back of Paige's throat like a waterfall. She knew when she opened her mouth, they would all spill out. She hoped it wouldn't be too much for Mrs. Cooke. "Well, I got that email you sent me, which was so sweet. And I have been having such a hard time dealing with this place and the reasons why I decided to come here. And then Eli and his daughter, Lucy, have begun to mean something to me. All of which is the long way of saying, I feel like if I let them into my heart, Christmas is going to win, and Paige Langford is going to lose."

Paige fell silent. She saw in Mrs. Cooke's face the signs of regret. She sprang from the couch and made ready to rush the door so she could get out of there without causing Mrs. Cooke any further embarrassment. "I'm sorry, Mrs. Cooke. I'll be leaving now." Paige headed to the door. If she had to, she would let herself out. Anything would be better than staying behind in that cabin considering how horribly she misread Mrs. Cooke's email.

"Paige Emily Langford." Paige stopped in her tracks and directed a look of extreme puzzlement at Mrs. Cooke. "Don't be silly. I followed you on Twitter, in addition to watching your podcasts and buying one of your books. I hear Twitter is not as cool as it once was, but I do like to hang out there 280 characters at a time. Anyway, your Twitter handle is replete with your middle name—that's where I got it from. My goodness, you looked at me like I was some sort of wizard." Mrs. Cooke rolled her eyes at Paige's silliness. "Oh, and please call me, Kelly. I don't think I can stand to hear you call me Mrs. Cooke any more than Daniel can stand to take a bath. Will you do that for me?"

Paige shook her head. "Yes," she said.

"Good." Mrs. Cooke patted the couch beside her the way a mother would. "Now, come on over here and we'll go through those problems of yours one at a time." Mrs. Cooke threw her hands into the air so they displayed a 'devil may care' attitude. "Or, we'll sort them into groups and deal with them by category. Either way, I'm not letting you leave my cabin until we figure out what is troubling you."

Paige walked back toward the couch. She allowed Mrs. Cooke to pull her down beside her. She felt she wanted to get the hardest part of this conversation out of the way first. It was just like what Lucy had gone through the day before when trying to explain the death of her mom to Paige. "I'm sorry, Mm…, Kelly. My parents died in a car crash when I was very young. Most of the time I think I've adjusted to the past, but every once in a while, mostly when I really want my mom and dad back, it overwhelms me. Something about the way you wrote to me made me think you understood how I was feeling."

Mrs. Cooke looked at Paige with no judgment. She did understand what it meant to be vulnerable without a good reason. "Oh Paige, I did sense you needed comforting. And I would be glad to be there for you. You might even say you could be there for me by letting me be there for you."

Paige was confused. "What do you mean?" she asked.

"Mr. Cooke and I lost our only child fifteen years ago this Christmas season." Paige could tell the revelation melted Mrs. Cooke a little on the inside. Her practiced aspect of being strong and fiery could not come close to drowning out the heart-breaking void in the center of her life. Paige could see she had learned how to ignore the pain, but she never learned how to unfeel it.

"Kelly, I'm so sorry." Paige imagined herself as a localized cloud of rain in Mrs. Cooke's otherwise sunny day. Why was she being so selfish all the sudden? It was not like her to think of herself before others. And yet, here she was, in this stranger's house, practically begging for a surrogate mother from someone who had lost a child. Paige hardly recognized this person she had become.

"Don't be. It's true what they say; time heals all wounds. When you live as long as I have beyond a tragedy you thought there was no way you could live beyond, you learn the truth of that famous saying." Mrs. Cooke inclined her head toward Paige the way people do when they think their next words are obvious. "In fact, the only thing truer than time healing all wounds is that other famous saying: that which doesn't kill you makes you stronger."

"I have that in a frame in my room in Los Angeles," Paige said.

Mrs. Cooke laughed. "Of course, you do. I have it in a frame in my room in Concord."

Paige leaned in to Mrs. Cooke and gave her a hug. It was the only thing she could do that might keep her from breaking out in sobs. "So, you see, don't you? I mean, if anyone can understand, it has to be you. My parents were on their way to a Christmas party the night they were hit by a drunk driver. There is a reason I can't let Christmas win, Kelly. It's because Christmas broke my heart."

"My dear, you have to open that heart back up. You have to let Christmas back in. You have to let people back in. I need to do that too. I feel like we've all been brought here for a reason. You, me, Daniel, Jessica, Eli, Lucy, probably Ian too. We all have something to learn from each other this Christmas, and it has to do with opening up our hearts."

Paige finally let go. She had carried these tears around with her for the better part of two and a half decades. It was the kind of soul-wracking crying that most often comes without noise. The only sound was the occasional catch in her breath as she went back into the well of her pain for another bucket of the past. Mrs. Cooke recognized this was exactly what Paige needed. So, she did what any mother would. She let her cry it out without making her feel as though she were weak for being sad. She knew from personal experience, sometimes it was best to uncork the sadness and let it pour. If you kept it locked away, it would get more and more bitter, until it passed from water into vinegar.

Paige's tears flowed until her environment provided her with a thick enough cue to get her to stop. In this case, it was the shutting off of the water in the bathroom where Mr. Cooke was taking his shower. Paige heard the faucet groan as Mr. Cooke closed the spigot. She determined there was a decent chance he would soon be back in the living room. Naturally, she didn't want him to see her in this condition, so she began to dab at her eyes. The first thing she thought to do once she regained control of her emotions was to apologize for her behavior. "I'm so sorry, Kelly." She reverted to a stock response for covering outbursts like hers. "I'm not sure what came over me."

Mrs. Cooke was having none of it. She knew exactly what came over Paige, and she wasn't about to let Paige paper it over with the usual excuses. "Nonsense." Obviously, this was one of her go-to responses when someone was trying to take blame, which wasn't theirs to take. "I know exactly what came over you. Honestly, I'm surprised it wasn't more. Your response is in proportion to the amount of pain you felt as a child." Mrs. Cooke imagined she would be able to do a whole lot more for Paige if she got all the information about Paige's loss out in one sitting. She knew you can't move past something if you don't get it out in the open. She also knew, like Paige, her husband would be making his way back to the living room soon. It wasn't that she thought he shouldn't hear what they were talking about; it was that she knew his male chromosomes would severely disturb the healing momentum she and Paige had developed together. She figured rapid-fire questions would be the best way to get to the heart of Paige's pain given the time constraints caused by the chances of her husband's reappearance. "How old were you?"

Paige's breath sputtered. She was in the aftereffects of The Big Cry. It would be a while before she was completely recovered. "I was six."

Mrs. Cooke's face mirrored Paige's pain. "That is such a young age to lose both parents. It's just awful. You still believed in things like the magic of Christmas and Santa Claus, didn't you?"

"I did."

"Where did you go?"

"My family had just moved to Los Angeles that summer. My Mom wanted to be an actress, and my Dad wrote screenplays. So, we didn't know many people." Paige's eyes began to mist up again. If not for the fact that she dreaded the idea of Mr. Cooke seeing her dissolved in a flood of tears, she would have let her emotions run free. "I was at my best friend's house the night it happened."

Paige paused for a moment. She tried to understand why she was overcome with this desire to unburden herself to Mrs. Cooke. In some hidden corner of her psyche, it seemed she just knew Mrs. Cooke would make her safe. And safe was exactly what Paige wanted to feel. "Of course, my best friend from then is still my best friend now."

"So, you stayed with Jessica and her parents." Mrs. Cooke put it all together. "There must be a wellspring of obligation pooling in that cistern."

"It took a few months for the courts to get on board." Paige shook her head at the memory. "I did spend a few weeks as a foster kid. But eventually, Bob, Glenda, and Jessica rescued me." Paige lowered her gaze to her lap. She felt so strongly the depth and breadth of their kindness. "I owe them all so much." It was that feeling of knowing how much she owed to the Keller family that had nearly brought her to tears a second time. How many nights of her life passed with her unable to fall asleep because her mind kept revolving around the idea that no matter what she did, no matter how she tried, she would never be able to pay the Keller's back for what they had done for her.

Paige heard the sound of drawers opening and

closing in the back room. Mr. Cooke, no doubt, finishing his post-shower routine. She felt the invisible clock ticking down on the last minutes of privacy before he reemerged. It made her nervous, not because she thought he'd judge her, but because whatever spell had allowed her to open up this far felt fragile, impermanent. Kelly's next words were careful, almost clinical. "You also mentioned Eli and Lucy were a source of trouble for you this Christmas."

Paige's breath caught. So, Kelly hadn't missed it. She had threaded that truth into their conversation earlier—more like confessed it, really—but she hadn't expected Kelly to loop back around and ask for clarity. It was such a delicate question, posed gently, but it reached into the very heart of what Paige had been trying to avoid. She hadn't entirely sorted it herself. What was Eli to her? What was Lucy? And more frightening: what was Christmas becoming? Kelly wasn't guessing wildly. Paige could tell from the tone. She had already formed a picture, but she wanted Paige to fill in the details herself. It didn't feel like interrogation. It felt like invitation. And Paige had no idea if she could do it.

"Yes," Paige stumbled through her answer. "Yes, I suppose they are… a source of trouble." Paige trusted Mrs. Cooke's phrasing was less revealing than anything she might come up with.

"And, I take it Lucy has let you know that she knows what it means to lose a parent." Kelly's words landed gently, but they pressed against Paige's chest like a stone. She heard the faint clatter of dresser drawers from the back bedroom and knew Daniel was finishing up. Paige sensed the moment's intimacy evaporating. This connection between them wouldn't last much longer.

He'd reappear soon enough, probably with a comment about the Patriots or Bill Belichick, and the room would recalibrate to something much less fragile. Kelly leaned in slightly, her tone shifting. "It's not fear of being a mother figure to Lucy that is causing the trouble, is it?"

Paige felt herself spinning. What wonderful and terrible feelings whirled inside her. Mrs. Cooke's question ripped open the secret trauma in her heart and caused it to bleed all over her. Of course, she was afraid. How could she ever let herself love someone the way her mom and dad loved her? How could she do that when she could not be sure she would always be there to protect them? Being a parent was the worst idea ever. It was founded on a lie that Paige could not support. If she could not always be there to love and care for the person that most needed love and care from her, then what was the point of being there at all?

Mrs. Cooke split Paige in two with her question. She also made it clear to Paige what she needed to do. "I hadn't really seen it before you pointed it out to me. But that is what the trouble is." Paige felt herself numbing. In her mind, she slipped away from Dayton, from Eli, and from Lucy. In her mind, she saw herself returning to Los Angeles. It was the right thing to do. There was no such thing as… Christmas at First Sight. Paige had never been so certain of anything in her life. She stood up. "Thank you for your time, Mrs. Cooke."

Kelly stood too, slowly. Paige wasn't sure what gave her pause. Maybe it was the flat edge in Paige's voice. The part that didn't sound like her at all. She didn't mean to sound robotic, but she felt herself shutting down. It wasn't Kelly's fault. It wasn't anyone's fault. That was just how this kind of clarity worked. It was blunt, cold and mechanical. "You don't have to rush off, Paige. I would love to visit with you some more. We can talk about whatever you want to talk about. We don't have to talk about the hurtful things."

When Mrs. Cooke ran her hands through Paige's hair, the way a concerned mother would, it was almost enough to break through the veil of indifference Paige draped over her emotions. *Almost.* "Tell Mr. Cooke I said bye." Paige walked toward the front door of the cabin. She didn't wait for Mrs. Cooke. She let herself out.

CHAPTER TEN

Moments like this are buds on the tree of life, flowers of darkness they are, she thought.

These words from Mrs. Dalloway fluttered through Paige's mind as the Los Angeles cab driver began to pull away before she even had the rear passenger side door of the cab closed. She stood in her driveway, filling with disgust as she watched him zoom off. She indicted his aggressive driving as decidedly unsafe for the neighborhood. Had he not noticed all the kids riding their bikes in the warm December air? "You are exactly what I think of when I think, Merry Christmas," Paige said to the receding taillights. She didn't want to be in a Christmassy mood, and for once the world cooperated with her. Virginia would agree. The few times she mentioned Christmas in her diaries, it had not been with any special luster.

The entire plan in going to New Hampshire had come crashing down around her after her visit with Mrs. Cooke. None of that meant she blamed Mrs. Cooke. She didn't even think it was her fault while not actively blaming her, a tactic routinely used by fundamentally damaged people. The reasons she left Dayton in such a hurry, and without properly saying goodbye to any of the nice people she met while there, were all her own.

Mrs. Cooke helped to uncover them, but she was not responsible for their creation.

What a mess she had made! Paige was sure her lifelong sisterhood with Jessica was in jeopardy for the first time. Jessica hadn't understood why Paige wanted to leave. On top of that, she was having too much fun to take Paige's word that the whole idea had been a mistake. In the end, both tempers flared. Things were said that would be hard for each to unsay. Paige's biggest regret came when she reminded Jessica, they weren't *actually* sisters, no matter how much Jessica tried to pretend like they were.

Of course, their argument hadn't progressed a word past that remark. Jessica stormed out of the common room, marched upstairs to her room, and slammed the door. If Paige remembered correctly, it was in the moment Jessica's door slammed shut that the first few tears began streaming down Lucy's face. Paige saw the glistening trails on the sides of Lucy's cheeks and lost her sense of perspective. She hammered her conscience for causing all these problems by not knowing beforehand that all these problems were going to happen the moment she accepted Mayor Turner's offer. Knee-jerk reactions were not usually a part of Paige's self-management style, but the degree to which she held herself responsible for all the terrible things happening in the world around her was not usual. She did what she thought she must. She called the first cab company Google suggested to her. She packed her stuff into her two suitcases and then disappeared down to the end of the lane to wait for the cab.

Paige imagined Jessica was upstairs in her room,

fuming at her. Eli was likely in Lucy's room, trying to put all the emotional fires out she had started in his young daughter. Mr. and Mrs. Cooke would be oblivious to everything in the safety of Cabin One. Ian was probably putting the finishing touches on the repair he and Jessica had spent all day working on… also caught in a sparkling oblivion. The result of this was that there was no one there to see her leave when she left. She was able to make some Christmas magic after all. She disappeared from all their lives.

She was somewhere over middle-America on the flight back to Los Angeles when the guilt began to sink in. Thankfully, her phone was off in observance of airplane flight rules. She didn't have to deal with the hundred text messages she knew she must be getting from Jessica for abandoning her. What had happened to her in New Hampshire? How had it happened so fast? It seemed to her as though she'd gone completely off the rails in slightly less than twenty-four hours. That kind of thing didn't happen to otherwise sane people. Paige always thought of herself as a reasonably stable person, so where had things gone so wrong?

During the flight, she used her laptop to draft apology letter after apology letter, one each for Eli, Lucy, Jessica, Mrs. Cooke, and Mr. Turner. By the time she touched down at LAX every single letter had been deleted. She didn't know what to say that would forgive her, her trespasses. It seemed like the best thing to do was to imitate an ostrich and stick her head in the sand until Christmas was over. After that, after she didn't have to be the sole arbiter of so many people's holiday, she could work out what to do to fix her damaged relationship with

Jessica. She loved Jessica. She would do anything in the world for her. It might take several months to erase the memory of abandoning her in New Hampshire, but Paige would succeed in the end. She didn't have a choice. You did whatever it took to make things up to your family.

As she watched the cab driver make a right at the stop sign, Paige wondered if that hadn't been the whole problem after all. Was her excessive desire to be right about Christmas, and to prove everyone else wrong, the cause of the disaster she wrought on Jessica and the people of Dayton? Mrs. Cooke reduced her to tears in the minutes before she left by forcing her to realize that her spite toward Christmas was really spite toward the world for taking her mother and father from her when she was barely six years old. Of course, the accident happened on the way to a Christmas party. Naturally, Paige's six-year-old mind associated the holiday with loss and eternal disappointment. An association that persisted into Paige's adult psyche.

Mrs. Cooke pointed this out for Paige while also hinting that the love developing inside her, for Eli and Lucy, was not something her soul would accept. She never realized, until her talk with Mrs. Cooke, how strongly she felt about not being a mother. It was strange for her to have to admit she was so petrified something would happen to take her away from her child —she didn't want to have children at all. Since losing a mother had already happened to Lucy once, Paige could not willingly put her in line for another dose. Even if the possibility of that dose was overwhelmingly remote. The world was unpredictable. It made no guarantees. How could Lucy deal with losing *another* mother? How could

Paige put her through the possibility of that?

As Paige wheeled her suitcases toward her house, she saw how ridiculous this all sounded when it was collected into paragraph form and available for general scrutiny. In other words, Paige knew she wasn't disqualified from trying to be a mother figure to Lucy because she couldn't promise the world wouldn't separate them before they were ready. Her rational grown-up mind knew this didn't disqualify her, at any rate. It was just the part of her that made the decision to leave Dayton without saying goodbye. That part of her was still a six-year-old kid sleeping over at her best friend's house for the first time.

She fumbled the keys to her house twice before she successfully got them in the lock and opened the door. As it swung inward, she felt the stale air greet her. The temperature while she was gone had been warmer than when she left. So warm, she instantly regretted turning the thermostat controls all the way off. The heat and humidity had collected in her tiny house like a sauna. Her emotional misery was complete. She could have done without the added physical nuisance of uncomfortable air. Once inside, Paige headed straight for that thermostat. She moved the little plastic dial from off to on and turned the temperature control down to fifty-five as well. Generally described as cold-blooded by those who knew her well, this intense fascination with getting her house cooler was not usual for Paige. She knew she was casting about for things to do that would keep her from doing the thing she had avoided ever since her plane landed at LAX. Namely, turning her cell phone back on and checking to see how much damage she had done.

She continued to search her darkened house for something which would keep her busy for a few more minutes. Nothing presented itself as a suitable distraction. The clock on the kitchen stove said it was just after 3pm. Paige resolved that at 3:15 she would turn her phone on and finally accept responsibility. Until then, she would continue to act as though nothing important had happened in her life over the last three days. It was a paltry compromise. One that was unlikely to last.

With little else to do but think, Paige sank into the easy chair parked beside the couch. Sitting there allowed her to view the shelf of books she had placed beside the TV. Of course, her shelf of books reminded her of the shelf of books in her room back in Eli's bed-and-breakfast, and how she had made so much psychological hay out of the books on that shelf. How she had turned them into harbingers of Eli's personality.

Her eyes slid off the bookshelf and landed on the suitcases parked by the front door. Had it cooled off enough in her house for her to tackle the prospect of unpacking? Maybe she should get her purse and finally turn that phone on? Both activities needed to be done soon. Paige tried to decide which one to undertake first by guessing which one would give her the least amount of guilt. She didn't get anywhere with this assessment because she got waylaid by the idea it depended on whether she meant guilt in the long or the short term. Obviously, her short-term guilt would be lower if she unpacked her suitcases. While unpacking, she wouldn't be checking her messages and emails from her loved ones. Necessarily, this would lead to far less short-term guilt, since those messages and emails were sure to be filled with heaping quantities of hurt feelings. However, her long-term guilt was going to continue to grow at a constant rate until whenever she did her duty and turned that phone on. She knew Jessica was sick with worry, and the longer she waited to quiet that worry, the greater her culpability for causing it would be. Paige was also sure Bob and Glenda had been interrupted on their vacation with the news Paige suffered some sort of emotional breakdown. The idea that they might think of leaving their cruise early to come check on her was the straw that finally broke the back of her indecision. She couldn't take it anymore. She went and retrieved her purse.

The phone didn't immediately fall out like it usually did. This forced Paige to open it wider than normal in order to look inside. It was then she saw the envelope. The one Vincent gave her in his office back in the Dayton county courthouse. Her heart seized with panic for at least the fifth time in the last couple of days. She realized she had forgotten her promise to Mr. Turner. He asked her to open the letter and read it whenever she knew for sure Dayton hadn't changed her mind about Christmas. That moment passed more than twelve hours ago. Yet, it slipped her mind to read the letter. How many more promises was she going to break before this miserable Christmas finally ended? How many more times was she going to have to think of herself as a terrible person for having accepted Mr. Turner's bargain in the first place? Good Lord, she hadn't even done it for herself! She did it for Jessica. Didn't that count for anything?

She pulled the letter from her purse while thinking about that old maxim about what the road to hell is paved with. She walked back to the easy chair and turned on the lamp that was positioned to cast the perfect amount of light on the area of the chair where a seated person would be likely to hold a book. She tore open the envelope and spilled its contents into her lap. It held a few sheets of paper stapled together and folded into thirds. Underneath this was another, slightly smaller, sealed envelope. Since the stapled sheets of paper were more accessible, she began there. The pages were addressed to her. She flipped to the last page of the document and saw it was signed by the mayor. In between was a double-spaced typed letter. Very much intrigued, Paige began to read.

Paige,

I hope you will forgive me for the artifice that brought you to my town. Please understand there were no official participants in the artifice other than me. Eli and Lucy, especially Lucy, had nothing to do with your invitation here. I am an old fool blinded by the idea that there is actual magic in Christmas. I know our senses tell us there is no possibility of truth in that statement, and still… I believe. If there is to be any blame accrued for the time you spend in Dayton, please ensure it is delivered to my address.

If all has gone according to plan, then you are reading this after we have met in my office and I have told you the town never put up any money to bring you here. I have covered the bill for all the expenses. I want you to know I entered into this willingly and as a testament to that silly belief I mentioned in the previous paragraph. It may sound ridiculous but, the truth is, I wanted you to come to Dayton and change your mind about Christmas.

Of course, if I had just been an old codger with an abiding love of tinsel and giant nutcrackers, our paths would very likely never have crossed. In addition to this, however, I am also the uncle of the wonderfully precious, Lucy. My wife is the older sister, by ten years, to Lucy's mom, Anna. Even if just these things had been true, you and I would have still been unlikely to meet. One additional element was needed to get the motion of our respective planets to cross paths. You will call this element coincidence or chance. I will call it fate, Christmas magic, or the work of an Angel.

As it turns out, my sister, Mrs. Teresa Atwell, is the seventh grade English teacher at Dayton Middle School. Yes, our community is as intertwined as it is close-knit. She came to me a few days after Thanksgiving with a "story" Lucy wrote as a homework assignment. Needless to say, you are here in my town because of the contents of that story. You are here in my town because of what the contents of that story did to this old codger's heart when he read it.

Of course, giving you this letter is a last-ditch effort. I had hoped that our love of the holiday would naturally infect you. I wouldn't have invited you if I didn't believe that somewhere in your heart the love of Christmas burns deeply in you. I certainly wouldn't have invited you if I thought you would make things worse for Lucy. As it is, I have listened to just about all of your podcasts. I even read all four of the books you wrote for middle-schoolers that Lucy loves so much. I know you fairly well; I think. You don't get elected mayor of Dayton, New Hampshire, for three consecutive terms without being a decent judge of people. What I see in my heart when I think of you is that you are a very good person, Paige Langford.

Enclosed is a copy of the assignment Lucy turned in to my sister. Please do me a favor and destroy it after you read it. I get the idea, from my sister, Lucy is quite embarrassed by her effort despite the fact my sister assured her it is several grade levels above where her writing should be for her age. As I noted at the beginning, she is precious.

I'll leave the rest to Lucy...

CHAPTER ELEVEN

Knowledge came through suffering.

The first quote she came up with, from her primary idol's best book, was of no solace whatsoever. True, yes. Solace, no. Paige needed something that would let her handle reading Lucy's story. Perhaps for the first time ever, Virginia Woolf had not soothed her. Whatever knowledge might come to her from reading Lucy's story, Paige was pretty sure would make her suffer, and she didn't want to. Not right now. Not with all the guilt she already felt. Since there was nowhere else handy to put it, she placed the envelope back inside her purse. She then dug around inside it until she found her phone. Could she handle the phone? Jessica had probably disowned her. No, she could not handle the phone either. She set that down on the table which held the reading light. She had to do something small before she ended up doing something drastic, like putting her house on the market and moving to the great state of New Hampshire.

All at once, she knew what she could do. She leapt from her easy chair and rocketed across the space to her front door. She grabbed her keys from the hook next to the coat rack and raced outside. She didn't even take the time to lock it behind her. She high-stepped from her yard over to Mr. Wyatt's. In her mind, she completed a quick prayer. She needed him to be home. There was no other option for her other than him being home.

The first few knocks on his door indicated she might be disappointed in her latest seat-of-her-pants plan. Finally, after what seemed an interminable amount of time to Paige, Mr. Wyatt answered. He wore head to toe velour fabric sweats in spite of the heat. He also had on his customary hair-killing hat. He must have looked at her through the peephole because he opened the door with a greeting which said he knew she was the one who knocked. "Good afternoon, Paige."

Paige managed to bite down on the desire, which was surging within her, to ask him how in the world he was wearing sweats in the overwhelming heat. She was so stressed her manners were taking a backseat to her anxiety. "Good afternoon, Mr. Wyatt." It was now Paige's turn to stand on Mr. Wyatt's porch, unable to say the things she had come over to say. Somehow going to New Hampshire for Christmas caused them to swap their customary roles.

Paige waited impatiently for Mr. Wyatt to rescue her by asking what she wanted. Eventually, he did. "What can I do for you, Paige?"

Moment of truth for Paige and her seat-of-the pants idea. Did she go through with it and ask him, or did she go back to her house and face that letter from Lucy and the phone in need of being turned on? She decided on asking Mr. Wyatt. "I was wondering if there was any chance..." Even though she committed to this course of action in her mind, now that she was at the point which would bring the moment to its crisis, she found her nerve ebbing. She closed her eyes and swallowed hard. "I kind of wanted to take you out to eat."

There, she said it. The ball was in his court. If he said yes, Paige figured she would get at least an hour, maybe an hour and a half, of respite from the problems she caused in her life. She hastened to add a few things she thought would sweeten the pot for him. "Your choice, of course. And we can take my car."

Mr. Wyatt eyed Paige skeptically. Of all the neighbors Mr. Wyatt had—left, right, and across the street—Paige knew she was the only one who didn't actively avoid him. It wasn't kindness, exactly. She just couldn't bring herself to treat him like a nuisance, no matter how rigid his rituals or how many times he made her move her car two inches to the left. If he noticed her civility, fine. But it wasn't goodwill. She wouldn't have thought of inviting him to dinner if it weren't for something more. The look in his eyes told Paige he was going to make her sweat it a little longer. "Why would you want to do that?"

It was a good question. Why did Paige want to do that? She couldn't give him the truth, could she? That he was the only person she knew who would answer the door on Christmas Eve and even think about accepting a spontaneous offer of dinner. Saying that smacked of rudeness as much as truth. She also couldn't tell him she would give anything not to be alone in her house with her cellphone and the story of an eleven-year-old. Instead, she went with the kind of white lie that often suffices as truth because it is so ordinary it could actually be true. "On the plane back from my business trip, I realized you had been settled in for several months now and I never did anything to welcome you to the neighborhood."

Paige saw it land. He seemed to think it would do in a pinch. His head bobbed once, slow and ceremonial. "Where I come from, we always greeted new people when they moved in with welcome baskets and fresh vegetables from the garden if they were in season. I retired here because I thought it would be pleasant, you know."

Relief showed on Paige's face. "Does that mean you'll come?"

Mr. Wyatt grimaced. "Well, I had just started that new Antman movie on Netflix." Paige bent her face in a way that pleaded with Mr. Wyatt to come out to eat with her. She was desperate enough to believe it was pushing him over the edge. She was right. "Okay. Okay. I'll go. Let me grab my coat."

Paige shook her head. Velour sweat suit. And a coat. In this heat. Mr. Wyatt was a whole different type of cold-blooded. She waited on his front porch while he found one of those light, Members Only, old-man jackets from a closet somewhere in the depths of his house. She thought he probably bought it back in 1987 and never mistreated it enough to wear it out. She still didn't know why it had occurred to her to come over here and ask him to dinner, but she was glad he had accepted. She had to run into her house to grab her purse and keys, while studiously avoiding her phone. It would still be switched off and sitting on the table beside the easy chair. Then, she and Mr. Wyatt could be on their way to the restaurant of his choice. As she was thinking this, he reappeared in the doorway with the keys to his own house in his hand. He joined her on the front porch as he pulled the door shut behind him. "One second to lock up and I'll be ready."

“Great.” Paige pointed to her driveway. “I’ll meet you at my car. I’ve got to grab my keys and lock up too.”

“Of course,” Mr. Wyatt agreed. “Take your time. Even in my youth, I wasn’t much of a sprinter.”

“Will do.” Paige hopped from Mr. Wyatt’s porch. She skipped back to her own house. Something about Mr. Wyatt’s acceptance of her offer of dinner worked to brighten her mood. It was as if she thought she was back to being fit for human consumption. Mr. Wyatt might not have been the highest bar to clear, but he was a start.

Inside her house, she grabbed her keys while managing not to think her cell phone was looking at her with scurrilous intent. The tendency to anthropomorphize everything in her life was always stronger in her than in most people. It was the main reason she gravitated toward being a writer. Her earliest memories involved making up stories about the objects in her parents’ house she had been attached to, but which disappeared after they disappeared. Her favorite involved a grandfather clock her Dad got from his actual grandfather. She used to think the space behind the glass where the pendulum swung was the perfect height for a girl of six to stand inside. Naturally, she made it into a kind of magical portal through which children could go and be reunited with lost families.

She wanted to tell the cell phone, with its scurrilously dark expression, to ‘take that’. If it knew what she had been through, it would not be the first to cast stones. Fortunately for her, Jessica did know what she had been through. She hoped it would be enough to salvage their sisterhood. In her heart, she believed it would be. It was her mind which struggled so mightily with belief. Paige frowned as she turned the lights off on the sleeping phone. She knew there was no one around to witness, so she risked a bit of craziness by addressing it directly. "You try believing in things you can't control when you get taught when you are six years old the things you can't control can jump up out of the dark and eat the people you love." Paige shut and locked the door to her house and then joined Mr. Wyatt in the front of her BMW. As she started the car, she asked, "So, where should we eat?"

Mr. Wyatt had a suggestion. Paige sensed he didn't want to give it because he didn't want to be judged. "I have an idea."

Something was holding Mr. Wyatt back from just coming out with his suggestion. Paige prompted him, "Great, let's hear it. I'm literally up for anything." In case that was not enough to convince him she would be totally open to suggestion, she added, "There is zero chance I will not agree to whatever you choose."

Mr. Wyatt considered the proposal. Paige could tell he still thought she might hold his choice against him. "You have to remember I've only been in Los Angeles a few months."

Paige put the BMW into reverse and idled down her short driveway right up to the cusp of pulling into the street. She couldn't fully commit to the maneuver because Mr. Wyatt hadn't expressed a location preference. She didn't know whether she should back into the street to the left or the right. "I promise to keep that in mind."

Paige would have been impatient with Mr. Wyatt's indecisiveness on any other day. She told him the choice was his, and she would happily go wherever that choice took them. This evening, however, Paige felt like the last person in first period to get invited to the homecoming dance. She would have waited for Mr. Wyatt to read the Declaration of Independence and half the Constitution before she would have considered putting any pressure on him to make the decision she had entrusted him to make.

Mr. Wyatt sighed. There was no more production he could make of his preference without falling into the territory of trying too hard to seem embarrassed. At a certain point, when a person keeps objecting that they don't want to make a spectacle of themselves, it becomes clear that, in fact, their greatest wish is to make a spectacle of themselves—a spectacle they hope the whole world is watching. "I really like the burgers at In-N-Out." Mr. Wyatt's confession left his head hanging in a shame, which was as palpable as he seemed to think it was legitimate.

Paige laughed out loud. "Oh my. You will get ZERO arguments from me on that one. I LOVE their burgers. And a good old-fashioned cheeseburger is exactly the kind of comfort food I need right now." Paige accelerated out of her driveway while cutting the wheel to the left. When she had sufficiently gained the lane, she slipped her car into drive and headed toward the stop sign at the end of the street. The same one the cab driver had been so eager to eclipse a half hour or so ago.

Paige saw that her warm embrace of Mr. Wyatt's dining choice had made all the difference. He relaxed and became a willing partner in the socialization Paige so desperately wanted from her fellow humans, without having to ask for it if possible. He began with the most recent thing she said, "Why comfort food?" It was the best clue she gave him as to why she would spontaneously invite him to dinner after having lived beside him in near-anonymity for over three months. Obviously, she needed comfort of some sort.

Regret bloomed in Paige for letting that little nugget slip out onto the floor of their conversation. She cast about for a rug to drag over it. "Oh, I always call it that." Paige watched as her false words sucked all the air out of the conversation. He knew she was lying. She saw him walling off his trust of her as a conversational partner. He switched to making his focus the cheeseburger, which waited for him at the end of the car ride.

"Oh yeah, I get that. We all do that, don't we?" Paige further intuited Mr. Wyatt was drawing back into himself like a turtle on an empty highway. Like that turtle, he knew there was nothing in his vicinity that was currently a threat to him. But, he also knew the topography was unsuited to turtles—at best—at worst, it was openly hostile. Better to be cautious than broken.

A crossroads. This was as true of her conversation with Mr. Wyatt as it was of her life in general. She had to decide whether she was going to live as an island unto herself or share her hopes, fears, and dreams with the people who chose to be around her. Perhaps, Mr. Wyatt was as good a place as any to start. "I do call it comfort food, but that's not what I meant when I said it."

Although she watched the road, she felt Mr. Wyatt turn his gaze back on her. "Feel free to tell me as much or as little as you want of your troubles. I know you're a good person, Paige."

Paige snorted slightly. "You know that's the second time I've heard those words in the last half hour. I'm not really sure they're true, especially the way I feel about myself right now."

"Something to do with the trip you just took?" Mr. Wyatt guessed. Paige shook her head, yes. She then filled Mr. Wyatt in on the backstory of her podcast. The term, podcast, needed several additional minutes of explanation before he was able to understand what it was Paige did on the internet. It wasn't until he suggested it was like an old timey radio show, and Paige agreed with that characterization, that they were able to move their discussion past the term. She then told him of the bet she had made with the mayor of Dayton, New Hampshire. The bet to see which of them would claim victory in a bout of Christmas Spirit versus Christmas Humbug. The traffic, as was usual for LA, was heavy so they made it through the introduction of all the important players in Paige's drama, Eli, Lucy, Jessica, Ian, and Mr. and Mrs. Cooke before they entered the parking lot of the In-N-Out.

She recounted the talk she had with Mrs. Cooke as they exited the BMW, entered the restaurant, and waited their turn to order. A few minutes later they were sitting in a booth by the window with generous servings of comfort food piled up before them. As Paige wound up her story, she gratefully realized Mr. Wyatt had been a wonderful listener. "I guess that's everything." Paige watched as Mr. Wyatt finished the fry he was eating and then reached for his soda to wash it down. Just when she was about to consider the possibility he had been a wonderful listener because he hadn't really been listening, he spoke up.

"That's a pickle for sure."

Paige assumed that would be all she got out of Mr. Wyatt. Maybe it was enough. It helped her to tell the whole story out loud. It let her see how the parts fit together. "Yeah, it is. Thanks..."

Mr. Wyatt shook his head; an indication Paige should quit talking. "I wasn't done."

"Oh no, of course, please go ahead." The stern way in which Mr. Wyatt invoked his conversational rights, intrigued Paige to hear what might follow.

"It seems to me like you ran away because you were afraid to face up to the fact that you were going to lose your bet. Like this idea of Paige Langford, the artist, author, podcaster, and hater of all things Christmas, was going to shrivel up and die if you had to admit there could be things in this world which you love even though they don't make sense." Mr. Wyatt paused to eat another French fry.

Paige, on the other hand, stopped eating. She wondered how many more times she was going to sit and talk with someone who could precisely pinpoint the inner workings of her psyche before this Christmas was over. She felt like she had entered an alternate dimension where everyone on the planet knew exactly how her brain functioned. In a nod to her writer's nature, part of her wanted to jot the idea down. There might be a future novel lurking inside that premise.

The French fry consumed; Mr. Wyatt picked up where he left off with the laser of perception he was aiming at Paige's motivations. "Also, I'm giving 10 to 1 odds you and this Eli fellow are perfect for each other. Since that wouldn't work unless you were also perfect for his daughter, the Christmas Spirit has seen fit to ensure you are. The three of you would, without a doubt, be a successful family."

The desire to interrupt flared in Paige. She felt like she couldn't let that one stand. She hadn't even known the Ryder's existed for seventy-two hours yet. How could it be possible Mr. Wyatt, who had never met them, knew Paige was perfect for them and they were perfect for her? "Mr. Wyatt..." Again, he held up his hand. Paige realized the things on his mind needed to be said in an uninterrupted way.

"One thing more before I stop my filibuster." Paige signaled she submitted to his request by remaining silent. "I'm just a retiree with a receding hairline and an obsession with lawn care." Paige smiled at the small jokes Mr. Wyatt made at his own expense. "But that doesn't mean I don't know what love looks like when I see it all over someone's face. You are one hundred percent, no doubt about it, in love with that man, his daughter, and their town."

Paige, who had been waiting patiently for her moment to speak so she could rebut all of Mr. Wyatt's comments with the cold inevitability of her omnipresent logic, suddenly found herself speechless. Words came to her in fits and starts, like a car in the first stages of running out of gas. "Mr... I... uh..." Paige gave up on any verbal momentum and concentrated on what she really wanted to say. It was like a lightbulb went off in her head. "My God!" Paige's eyes widened to the size of small saucers. "Mr. Wyatt, I see very clearly now that you are completely right."

Mr. Wyatt dissolved into an enormous grin. Paige imagined that living alone didn't offer a whole lot of chances to hear those words from others. She thought he looked quite proud of himself and needed an extra ounce of convincing. "I am?" he asked.

"You are." All at once, the brightness which infiltrated Paige's face while that lightbulb had been going off, dissipated. She was suddenly feeling very worried. "The question is, what do I do now. I really messed things up by leaving the way I did. I haven't known Eli long, but I do know he is very protective of his daughter, with good reason too. He doesn't want to take a chance on letting her get hurt if he can help it. She's already been through so much. I don't know if he would trust me after I ran out on them the way I did."

"When you go back, and believe me, you need to go back, you will have to explain to him why you did what you did. Give him credit. He will understand. Besides, we forgive a lot in those we love." Paige thought Mr. Wyatt said this as if he knew it from firsthand experience.

"But I don't know he loves me." Paige heard herself saying these ridiculous things and cringed. She had to stop before more of Mr. Wyatt's simplistic thinking infected her brain. "We have only been around each other for twenty-four hours. You can't fall in love with someone in a single day!" Paige's voice raised when she said this. It wasn't because she was mad at Mr. Wyatt, it was more like she was so incredulous about having to say sentences like that out loud. A few people in the In-N-Out looked sideways at her for disturbing their enjoyment of their own comfort food. Paige didn't care. She had to get this conversation steered back onto the ground of reality.

"Oh, I see." Mr. Wyatt looked to Paige like an inverse lightbulb had just gone off in his head. The kind of idea that makes things darker rather than brighter.

"You see what?" Paige demanded.

"Of course. I should have guessed from the beginning. We would have gotten much further in our conversation by now."

Mr. Wyatt's face mirrored what Paige imagined parents looked like when they admitted one of their children had failed to develop their most prized social belief. "What are you talking about, Mr. Wyatt?"

"Well, you don't believe in Christmas either. So, I suppose it all makes sense."

The impulse to know what Mr. Wyatt was actually talking about finally exceeded Paige's ability to resist. She needed to know what he was referring to. She would have to just flat out ask him. "All what makes sense, Mr. Wyatt? It sounds exactly like me, but, please, tell me what you're talking about? I don't understand."

"You don't believe in love at first sight, do you?" My Wyatt asked this as though it were the plainest, most unadorned question in the world. He asked it like he was asking about going to the grocery store or washing the sheets.

For the second time in as many minutes, Paige was at a loss for words. *Of course*, she didn't believe in love at first sight. She also didn't believe in unicorns or Santa Claus either. She didn't believe in any of those things because, like the rest of the grown-up world, she had stopped believing in fairy tales when she was a child. For the record, she stopped believing in fairy tales when she was six. How to put that sentiment into words without being quite so blistering… that was the challenge. "No, I don't. Do you?"

Mr. Wyatt's expression showed that he deeply considered her question. It was clear he did believe in love at first sight and was about to say so emphatically. Paige guessed the hesitation surrounded a desire to express his belief in a way he thought her hyper-logical thinking patterns would not automatically discount. After several moments of intense deliberation, Mr. Wyatt hit upon, what he seemed to think, was the perfect way to say it. "Judging by your vocabulary and the repeated mentioning of the fact that Virginia Woolf is your literary idol, I'm going to guess you are familiar with the British philosopher David Hume."

Paige wasn't sure how to take that one. "I don't know if you mean that as a compliment or an insult but, yes, I am familiar." Paige wanted to say that Hume's critique of the principle of sufficient reason was the main buttress against all arguments about impossible things, like love at first sight. What could Mr. Wyatt be driving at in bringing him up?

"Do you know what he said about miracles?" Mr. Wyatt asked.

Again, Paige was familiar. She didn't have it hanging in her room like she did with the quote Mrs. Cooke shared with her, but that was because it was not nearly as quotable as the thing Mrs. Cooke said about that which does not kill us. Paige decided on the less than ten words, Jessica-approved, bumper-sticker version.

"Basically, he said, if he witnessed a miracle, he would call himself crazy." As she had done with Eli, she counted her words. She managed to keep it exactly to ten. She left out the 'then' to do it. Plus, she didn't count the 'basically' and the 'he said', but that all seemed grammatically defensible to her. Score one for Paige's intellect.

"That's a very good summary of the main point of his argument. I like that." Mr. Wyatt fell silent. The silence went on so long, Paige wondered if he had decided against sharing what he was going to say.

She helped him out by connecting his dots in the way she thought they should be connected. "Are you saying I am right not to believe in love at first sight because if I did, I would have to call myself crazy?"

"Oh Lord, no. I'm sorry, my dear. I thought what I meant would be obvious, especially after that wonderfully concise summary you provided." Mr. Wyatt crumpled up the wrapper that had held his cheeseburger. "I was saying the polar opposite. I suppose I was trying to get you to see that being David Hume would have to be the most lifeless, penniless, leaden, existence imaginable." When Mr. Wyatt shook his head wistfully, Paige imagined he was running through the details of what it would be like to go through life not believing in anything you couldn't prove with a slide rule and a compass. "Whatever you do with your life, whatever you become, make sure it is not being David Hume. Belief makes life worthwhile."

Paige counted the words in Mr. Wyatt's maxim. Four. In general, the truer something was, the less words it took to say it. Four words was near the lower limit of where you could say something meaningful and have it be true. Two words was the absolute lower boundary, but Paige knew most two-word sentiments were boring even if they were true. "How do I not be David Hume, Mr. Wyatt, when it's all my life has taught me to be."

Mr. Wyatt laughed. An indication the prescription for his truth was as easy as it was self-evident. "You have to believe."

A distracted silence swallowed Paige whole. Her mind burned through fuel trying to process the implications of Mr. Wyatt's cure for her loneliness. That's what this was all about. Everything that happened to her on the trip tied directly to the unmitigated feeling of loneliness which sat in the pit of her stomach. She never talked about it, but it was always there, like her shadow on a cloudless day. "I don't know how to believe." The words left her of their own volition. The reasoning parts of her brain temporarily ceded control to the feeling parts. Paige was just along for the ride. She would keep riding those feelings until Mr. Wyatt brought her all the way to the station.

"Oh yes, you do. Everyone does. It's not a skill you learn, like riding a bike. It's part of what makes you human. You believe right now. You just choose to believe in the wrong things. You believe life is a desert with no possibility of oasis. You believe that connection with people who feel as deeply and as beautifully as you do is not real. You believe it is better to let the characters you write about, and read about, feel things for you. You believe you do not deserve to be loved." Mr. Wyatt's words pierced Paige's heart, much the same way Mrs. Cooke's words had pierced her heart earlier. She felt her eyes swelling with tears. She was out in public now. She couldn't let this happen to her.

Of course, it happened to her anyway. As she dissolved into tears, all the things she held inside since her childhood came flooding up to the surface of her mind and leaked into the world through her eyes. Her vision became so blurred with tears, she could not see. Mr. Wyatt saw what was happening to Paige and didn't hesitate. He jumped up from his side of the booth and traversed the space to her side. The big hug that enveloped her helped. She made a mental note to really thank him later, when she was not this silly person who kept turning into a bucket of tears in the company of near-strangers. "I'm sorry, Mr. Wyatt." Paige managed between gulps for air. "I'm not normally like this."

Mr. Wyatt continued to soothe her as best as he could. "Listen," he began, "I unapologetically believe in all those clichés cultured people from high-brow schools frown on as unwarranted wish fulfillment. They shuffle most of my favorite things into the category of superstition. Things like, 'love at first sight', 'life is beautiful', and that quintessential of all dime a dozen dogmas, 'everything happens for a reason'. People with fancy degrees and really wordy thesis papers will call me a fool, but I know I'm right. You don't have to believe it yourself right now. It will be enough, for now, if you let me believe it for you." Mr. Wyatt stopped hugging Paige for a moment so he could look her in the eyes. "Will you trust me on that piece?"

Paige ran a napkin underneath her nose, "Yes," she agreed.

"Good." Mr. Wyatt nodded his head once to show he was happy to have her consent on that point. "Now, I need you to agree to do two more things for me. I don't want you to think about it, or argue with me about it, or even think about whether you want to argue with me about it. I want you to just say you're going to do it. Can you do that too?"

Paige nodded her head, yes. "I can," she said.

Mr. Wyatt wasted no more time on preambles. He got right to the points he needed Paige to hear. "Number one, you must call your mom and dad. You must do it immediately. As a corollary, you must never call them 'Bob and Glenda' ever again. You deserve their love, and from what you've told me about them, I'm sure they want to give it to you." Mr. Wyatt talked right over the hiccup in Paige's speech. She was happy he did. Otherwise she might have broken down in tears again. "For the rest of your life, never doubt they love you as much as they love their own daughter. Never doubt you love them as much as you loved your biological parents. All of you deserve that peace. Take it, Paige."

Paige's head began to swim. How did Mr. Wyatt know so much about her life based on the summary she gave him on the drive over? "Who are you?" She had to say something to combat the spinning sensation his words caused in her. The depth and clarity with which he saw into her life on the basis of such inconsequential information astonished her.

"All my life my job has been to listen to the things people really want. When you've been doing it as long as I have, you get good at reading between the lines." Mr. Wyatt looked to Paige like he didn't want to elaborate anymore on how he came by his secret ability, like he just wanted to return to the second thing on his list of demands for her. "Number two, you have to read Lucy's story. You also have to do that right now." He must have realized he had now asked her to do two things at the same time. He rolled his eyes at himself for being confusing. "Okay, read the story first, then call your parents."

Paige used her eyes to plead with Mr. Wyatt the way a child might. She needed reassurance. "Are you sure it's going to be okay?"

"Everything will be fine." Relief flooded Paige, until Mr. Wyatt held up the index finger on his left hand. "On one condition."

She had to ask, even though she thought she knew the answer. "What is it?"

"You believe." Mr. Wyatt eased his way out of the booth seat he shared with Paige. He addressed her again from the head of the table. "It's a beautiful evening. I think I will go outside and enjoy the sun and breeze while you take your time reading through that story of Lucy's."

Mr. Wyatt walked toward the front of the restaurant. Paige jumped up after him. She stopped him before he managed to get five feet from the table. She wrapped him in an enormous bear hug. "Thank you so much for everything you've done for me in the last two hours. I'm not sure who you are, or how you know so much, but I am forever in your debt."

"There are no debtors where I come from, Paige." Mr. Wyatt gracefully ended the embrace. "Now, go and do those two things before you lose your nerve."

Paige returned to her booth. She watched Mr. Wyatt disappear outside in the general direction of where she parked. That would definitely go down as the strangest conversation of her life. She didn't know how Mr. Wyatt put so much together about her from the snippets she told him, but she was, in this moment, very motivated to do the things he suggested she do. She reached into her purse and pulled out the envelope with Lucy's story in it. As she did, she felt confident that she had told Mr. Wyatt about the story but had not told him it was still in her purse. Had she told him? She couldn't remember for sure. How had he known if she hadn't told him?

Paige unfolded Lucy's manuscript and looked at the pretty cursive script that only an eleven-year-old could take the time to write in. Her story was called King Christmas. Paige thought that was a great title. Lucy captured her attention from the start the way any writer hopes to do. Before settling in to read, she looked at the parking lot one last time. She tried to catch sight of the incredible Mr. Wyatt. An idea was beginning to poke at her mind the way a pebble pokes at your toe when it gets stuck in your shoe. She couldn't shake it. She hadn't told him she had brought the story with her.

She wound the time backward in her mind looking for the spot when she talked about the story. They were sitting at a traffic light, which had a gas station on the left and a fast-food chain on the right. She told him about the connections between Lucy, Mrs. Atwell, and Mr. Turner. She remembered telling him about being in her hot house staring at the envelope... and that was it. Now that she was putting her full attention on the problem, she was absolutely sure she hadn't mentioned she brought Lucy's story with her. Paige sighed. She accepted the fact that nothing which happened this Christmas was going to have a clear-cut answer. Right now, what she needed to do was read Lucy's story. She consoled herself by thinking Mr. Wyatt must have made a lucky guess.

She wasn't ready to believe… yet.

CHAPTER TWELVE

King Christmas

One day an old man went walking down by the sea. When he got to the place where the sea should be, he found it wasn't there anymore. "What have you done with my sea?" he asked the sky. But the sky would not answer him.

In the sandy distance he saw a blue pelican walking on one good leg and one bad leg. The old man thought a blue pelican with one bad leg would be the perfect thing to ask about a missing sea, especially since the sky would not answer him. So, he hurried as fast as he could in the blue pelican's direction.

Unfortunately, the old man had to follow the blue pelican for hours. It had a big head start, and he was an old man, so it was hard for him to catch up. The sun was awful bright on the white sandy beach and the old man's eyes hurt and his skin was burned by the time he finally caught up to the pelican with one good leg and one bad leg. It made him mad he had to walk so far on the hot sand and in the bright sun. He didn't talk to the blue pelican in a pleasant voice to begin with. "Blue Pelican, what have you done with my sea?" the old man demanded.

The old man's tone startled the blue pelican. "I have done nothing with your sea," the blue pelican said. "I am on my way to see King Christmas about my one bad leg, though. Maybe he can help with your missing sea problem."

The old man continued to be gruff, "My missing sea is everyone's problem. It's not just my problem."

"Then you should see King Christmas. He is very good at solving everyone problems," the blue pelican said sweetly.

"I do not like this King Christmas. He sounds like a busybody to me," the old man said.

"Suit yourself. I am on my way to see him about my problem leg, and I thought you could ask him about your problem sea, since he is good at solving everyone-type problems."

"I do not like this King Christmas, but I will go with you in case he has the answer." The old man assumed the blue pelican was crazy in addition to having one bad leg, but he didn't think it would hurt to put this King in his place if he got the chance. So, he began to walk beside the blue pelican on his quest to find King Christmas.

Along the way the old man told the blue pelican about how much he loved his sea. How beautiful she was when the sun sparkled on her. How she was even more beautiful at night when the moon sparkled on her. The old man did not understand how anyone could take his sea away from him since she was so big and so beautiful and so necessary.

They had been walking for several more hours when they came across a few shoots of an orange flower the old man knew from the country where he had been born. It would help to heal the blue pelican's bad leg problem. The old man stopped and told the blue pelican about the orange flower. "Blue pelican, if you will let me, I can make you a compress from this orange flower which will help to heal your wounded leg."

"I wanted King Christmas to heal my leg," the blue pelican began, "but it hurts me so much I will try your orange flower cure."

The old man made his compress and put it on the Blue pelican's bad leg. The two new friends sat in the blinding sun while the orange flower worked its magic. The old man told the blue pelican more stories about how much he missed his sea. The blue pelican agreed the sea must have been quite special.

After a while longer, the blue pelican felt much better. He thanked the old man for his orange flower cure and told him he would not be going to find King Christmas anymore since the old man cured him. He told the old man to say hi to King Christmas when he found him. The blue pelican wished the old man luck in finding out where his beautiful sea disappeared to.

The old man and the blue pelican parted ways as very good friends.

The old man continued walking through the blinding white sand. It seemed like days passed but he knew it was only hours. Eventually, he saw a lion who walked in circles as though he were blindfolded. The lion scared the old man, but every time he tried to walk around him, he changed direction, so their paths were destined to cross again.

Finally, the old man tired of trying to walk around the lion. He went right up to it. "Lion, do you know what happened to my sea. She is beautiful, and lovely, and sparkles in the sun and the moonlight."

The lion sniffed the air. "I don't know anything about a sea. I am looking for King Christmas. Only he can take my blindfold off. Seas do not matter where blindfolds are concerned."

"I am on my way to find King Christmas too. Maybe we can walk together," the old man said.

"You are not afraid to walk with me. Most men are scared to be near me." The lion was curious if the old man was like most men or not.

"I am old. I have lost my sea. Nothing will keep me from making it to King Christmas, and that is why I am not afraid of you. I will eat you if you try and keep me from knowing where my sea has gone.

The lion laughed at the old man's threat. "In that case, I would love to walk beside you on our way to find King Christmas.

The old man and the lion walked and talked until the day passed into night. The old man regaled the lion with more stories about his precious sea. How she provided him with all the food he needed to eat. How the rivers which fed her and kept her strong gave him the water he needed to drink. In short, his sea gave him life. He did not know what he would do now that she was gone.

The lion agreed this was a tough problem. He told the old man he was right to seek the help of King Christmas. He was the wisest man in the land. If anybody could help solve the missing sea problem, it was him.

After that, the old man and the lion talked about the blindfold which kept the lion from knowing where he went. The old man wanted to know where it came from.

"I don't know. I was asleep one night, and when I woke up, there it was. Many have tried to remove it, but none have

succeeded. I met a blue pelican some miles back the road who walked with a limp and told me about King Christmas. He said he could do anything. He had been on his way to see The King himself when a quiet old man healed him with a compress from an orange flower. Now, I am on my way to the King so I may be healed."

The old man leaned in close to the lion. He realized, because of the blindfold, the lion could not tell he was the old man from the blue pelican's story. "Do you mind if I give it a try?"

"I don't mind, but I doubt it will work. Countless others have failed. Only someone as powerful as King Christmas would succeed." The lion thought it was foolhardy to try but he also didn't think it would hurt much either.

The old man bent closer to the lion until his lips were grazing the fur which lined the inside of the lion's left ear. "Friend lion," he said, "the only blindfold on your eyes is the one you gave them." The old man rubbed the area around the lion's eyes on the top of his head, and then around both sides of his nose.

The lion spoke in a frantic voice. "I don't know what is happening. There are colors now. Blurry, but still colors. Each moment they are sharpening in detail." The lion turned his head to the old man. "I can see you," he said. "You are a magician!" He exclaimed. "You are the old man the blue pelican spoke of. You are the equal to King Christmas! I shall proclaim it through all the land. I will make you famous for your healing powers. First you cured the blue pelican and now you've cured me."

The old man interrupted the lion in the middle of his soliloquy of praise. "I am nothing but an admirer of a missing sea. I will give King Christmas your regards when I find him." The old man didn't want to be rude, but it was time he moved on. He had already been traveling for two days and there was no sign of his sea or King Christmas.

The days turned into weeks, followed by months, and, finally, years. The old man grew older still, but he would never stop walking and he never stopped believing he would one day find his missing sea. He knew it was out there somewhere beyond the next horizon, over the next hill of brilliant white sand.

He made many new friends on his travels, but none of them had seen his sea, and none of them brought him any closer to King Christmas. In every instance, he was able to help each of them. It seemed everyone in this land of his was in need of some kind of help. After a time, he began to look forward to it. It reduced his own pain, in not being able to lay his eyes upon his beautiful sea, to help others through their bad moments.

Many, many years after he began his journey, he came upon an extremely old blue pelican who had a scar on his leg in the same place as the one he had first helped all those years ago. He found him in the night on the side of the road, shivering in the cool night air. The old man nestled beside him to warm him since there was no fire.

The blue pelican awoke with a start when the first rays of the morning sun glanced off his feathers. He recognized his friend, the old man, but was surprised to see him still out wandering. "Old man, friend from many years gone by" the blue pelican began, "why are you still out here in the desert? Why haven't you gone home yet?"

The old man remembered the blue pelican had a way of

making him cross, but the years had taught him patience and compassion for others, so he met the blue pelican's question with practiced calm. "I haven't found my sea yet. And I miss her so desperately." The old man let his head fall in failure. "I never met King Christmas either. I feel I have wasted years of my life looking for things I don't even know for sure ever existed."

The blue pelican tried to respond, but his breath was taken by a series of horrible coughs. He accepted a canteen from the old man and took several sips of water. Eventually, he was able to speak without his cough interrupting him. "Would the journey be better, worse, or the same if they never existed?"

The old man thought about this for several moments. He wanted to give an honest answer. "I suppose it would be the same. Starting with you I made many friends while I was on my journey. I was able to help all of them because I knew so well what it meant to lose something. I gave a piece of myself to every person I met along the way. In doing that, I felt better about having lost my precious sea."

The blue pelican nodded. "I remember the sea you lost, and she was beautiful. There is only one way the world can be as beautiful as it was before she left it."

"What is that?" The old man desperately wanted to know.

"If you never stop telling everyone you meet how beautiful she was."

The old man broke down in tears. "But I loved her so much and I miss her so much."

"And by doing those things, you replace the light in the world that was lost when she was lost." The blue pelican was

again overcome by a terrible coughing fit. It took him a long time to recover. "Will you promise to do those things for me?"

"Of course, I will." Suddenly the old man was seized by a strange thought. "Who are you? I mean, who are you really, besides being the blue pelican?"

"I am King Christmas. I give lost souls what they need instead of what they want. When I saw you, I knew you wanted me to give you back your lost sea, but that was not in my power to give. So, I gave you the power to find her on your own... in your memories of her." The blue pelican then coughed so long the old man knew he was not long for this world.

"What do I do now?" The old man asked. "I spent so much time searching for my lost sea, I don't know who I am anymore."

The blue pelican smiled, faintly. "You are my heir. The king is dying and will soon be dead. Long live The King."

"I am not King Christmas."

The blue pelican pulled himself together to give his last words to this world. "Isn't that what the fellow travelers you meet call you when they meet you now? Don't they seek you out when you are walking near their homes and towns?"

The old man admitted this was true with a nod of his head.

The blue pelican was dying. He could feel himself lifting toward the sky. He had one more thing he wanted the old man to hear. "Whenever you give of yourself, you are King Christmas, and the sea you lost shines beautifully from within you."

The End

CHAPTER THIRTEEN

Paige cried so much while reading Lucy's short story that there was now a giant pile of napkins in the center of her table that she had used to dry her eyes and nose. She was also pretty sure at least one of the patrons of the In-N-Out considered calling rescue personnel to deal with her obsessive teariness. Of course, the actual story written by Lucy had not been 'the whole story' either. At the end of King Christmas, she added a personal note to her teacher, Mrs. Atwell. That was the part that really got to Paige.

Lucy's note started by telling Mrs. Atwell she was sorry she had gone so far over the page count requirements for the assignment, but the story kept growing in her mind as she wrote it. She also wanted Mrs. Atwell to know she had used all the vocabulary words from that week's word study, as outlined in the 'extra credit conditions'. The interesting part for Paige was when she confessed to having borrowed her main character's dilemma from one of Paige's books for young readers. Naturally, Paige recognized the old man's motivating desire to find something he lost that no one else believed existed as having strong parallels with her series, Broken Vessels, but not to the plagiaristic degree Lucy worried about. It was flattering, not copying. It was also disarming when Lucy told Mrs. Atwell she would rather get a zero on the assignment, or completely redo the assignment, then live with the idea she stole anything from her favorite author's work.

Lucy's note also made it clear she thought both stories, her own and Paige's, were tributes to the parents they lost as young children. She told Mrs. Atwell, and thanks to the efforts of her uncle, the mayor of Dayton, she also ended up telling Paige as well, that she felt like Paige's books were a gift from God when she needed one most. The books helped her feel grounded in the world on days when she thought she might just float away. Even in the note she made it clear Eli was the best dad ever, but every daughter wants a mother too. Paige knew what it felt like not to have one, and that made Paige so important to Lucy she wanted to honor her the only way she could think of, by writing her a story that was, at least in theory, based on Paige's own work.

And there were so many things in Paige's life Lucy's short story uncovered. She wouldn't allow herself to ignore them anymore. However, Mr. Wyatt gave her two directives, and she was determined to follow through on both of them. So, Paige folded up Lucy's story and fit it back into its envelope. She placed the envelope in her purse and picked up her trash. She dumped this and then went up to the first person she saw standing in line. Mr. Wyatt had been right with the first task he gave her; she wouldn't risk waiting until she got home to complete the second. The burly man with no hair on his head and more than a year's worth of hair on his face looked surprised, even beneath the beard, when she tapped him on the shoulder and asked to use his phone to call her parents.

He obliged her without thinking.

Paige dialed her mom's number even though she knew she'd be unlikely to answer given there was no chance she'd recognize the number. Besides, she was on vacation. She might not even have her phone turned on. As Paige predicted, the call went straight to voicemail after a single ring. She was prepared for this. She didn't even care that the burly stranger was going to hear every word.

"Mom," she began, "if you can please get Dad beside you and listen to this message on speakerphone, because it is meant for both of you, I would really appreciate it." Paige paused for a few moments to give her mom time to do those things if she could. "I need you guys to know you have been the best mom and dad to me that any girl could ever ask for. It's not fair of me to hold back parts of my love, or to call you 'Bob and Glenda' the way I sometimes do as though you were inferior to other people's parents just because you weren't related to me by blood. Even if my biological mother and father came back to life tomorrow, you two would still be my Mom and Dad. You are the ones who raised me. I am who I am because of you. And, I love you two with all the love I'm capable of." Paige paused again for a moment to compose herself. This message wasn't the place for tears. "That's it. I'll call you later from my regular phone... long story I don't have time for... but I just wanted you guys to know, right now, that I love you." Paige ended the call and handed the phone back to the burly stranger.

He took the phone and gave her a spontaneous hug. "I'd pay a million dollars for either of my boys to call me and say something like that."

Paige laughed. "Thank you for letting me use your phone. I've got to go because there are a bunch of other people who need an apology from me." With that, Paige darted out the front doors of the In-N-Out, expecting to run directly into Mr. Wyatt.

Once in the parking lot, Paige was frustrated by the fact she couldn't find him anywhere. Her frustration wasn't directed at him. She was mad at herself for leaving Jessica and all the good people she met in the town of Dayton without saying goodbye. She was getting on the next plane back to New Hampshire, no matter when it was due to leave. Of course, this plan would be in a holding pattern until she tracked down Mr. Wyatt and got him safely back to his house. Not until she circled the restaurant twice, did she get close enough to her car to read the note Mr. Wyatt had left under the driver's side windshield wiper. In it he thanked her for the lunch and told her to carry out whatever plans she made without worrying about getting him home. It was a nice evening, and he was in the mood to take his time getting back. Since he was already out, he wanted to have another adventure or two before the sun set on this beautiful day. Paige was sad she didn't get to thank him for what he had done for her or tell him she followed his instructions on both counts. She consoled herself by remembering he was, after all, her neighbor. When she got back from spending the rest of Christmas in New Hampshire, she would take him out to eat once a week until whenever they weren't neighbors anymore.

Paige started her car and pulled out onto the boulevard that would take her home, enjoying, for once, the snarling Los Angeles traffic. She had her windows down, and the sun was beating on the arm which rested on the sill of the door. The heat in her arm reminded her to be present in her life again. She would stop being a passenger who was surveying her life as it passed like a character in a mediocre book. She would be decisive. She would believe in things again. She would start with the mess she made in New Hampshire and work outward, in widening circles, from there. It felt good to have her course of action settled. It felt good to know she wasn't in danger of dissolving into tears before the traffic light in front of her turned green. Yes, she wanted to be in the air and headed back to the East Coast, but there was a certain amount of peace in being stopped up in this jam of human transport. It felt to her like a sea of tranquility in the middle of an ocean of turbulence.

The thought stuck in her mind. It felt true. Eli and Lucy and New Hampshire were what she wanted. Forever. Mr. Wyatt was right. The world was wrong. There was such a thing as love at first sight. She was sure Eli felt it too. There was no way that much electricity could flow between them and there not be something real beneath it. She remembered how right it felt when she gave him that soft kiss on the cheek, how much she wanted to turn her lips to his and kiss him properly. If someone gave her the chance, she would have wagered the deed to her house he felt the same way.

Those thoughts were hard to process in the middle of a Los Angeles traffic jam, so Paige chased them away for the time being. She would do what she needed to do if Eli and Lucy would even let her back in their lives. If she was right and what happened between her and Eli was really one of those once-in-a-lifetime things, then the details would work themselves out. As she turned onto the street that ran in front of her house, she thought she had never believed anything as strongly as she believed the truth in that last thought. Just like Mr. Wyatt said, she needed to believe in something in order to feel better. She chose to believe in Eli, Lucy, Christmas, and New Hampshire. And now, she did feel better. She would never give it up. She felt blessed and strong and lucky. The loneliness Lucy described so perfectly in her story King Christmas was no longer with her. If Eli and Lucy would let her, she would do whatever it took to scrub it from Lucy's world too.

It was as her hopes for Lucy coursed through her mind that she saw a literal miracle. Her conversation with Mr. Wyatt was prophetic. Here she was being confronted with an actual miracle. The choice was to believe it or call herself crazy. What choice would she make? She put her turn signal on and let her front tire fade into the grass in approximation of that grass-killing maneuver which brought Mr. Wyatt into her orbit to begin with. She put her car in park and glanced through the window, her face a mask of apprehension.

Since she worried she lacked the strength to stand, she let him open the door for her. She offered no resistance when he extended his big, beautiful hand into the cabin of her BMW and wrapped it around the muscles in her arm. Paige thought she might melt as he pulled her into his arms… and gave her the kiss that promised all of his love—at first sight. When their lips finally parted, she imagined she resembled one of those characters in those books about vampires, right after the bite which drained almost all their blood away. Dizzy wasn't adequate. Drained was as close as she could come to representing it.

It was the word she used when she told the story to Jessica later that evening.

"I'm sorry about that, Paige," Eli said. He looked as though he were actually upset with himself for risking a kiss before they talked.

Paige put her finger on his lips to quiet him. Then she gave him another kiss. The experience was one of freefall from thousands of feet without a parachute. It made her knees threaten to stop supporting her. Ultimately, she reasoned she would have to stop all this kissing or else risk physical injury owing to metaphorical syncope. "Why did you come?" she asked when the kiss ended.

"Mrs. Cooke came and talked to us after we found your note. I won't deny I was a little upset at first." He closed his eyes as if thinking about how true his next words were. "I was upset, for me, to be sure. I won't deny that. I feel a stronger connection to you than to any other person I've ever met, except Lucy's mom. But, way more importantly, I was upset for Lucy." Eli studied the ground for a moment. "Even though you barely know me, you have to know I wouldn't let anything hurt her—no matter what that thing meant to me. Lucy idolizes you. Your leaving without saying goodbye was going to be a hard thing to explain."

"I know that, Eli. All of it." Paige wanted to say a whole novel's worth of things after that tiny sentence, but she could tell Eli wasn't finished, so she silenced herself to let him complete his thoughts.

"And then Mrs. Cooke came up to the house to check on you. When you weren't there, she filled me in on most of the details of the conversation you had with her before you left." Paige could tell Eli felt bad about the talk he shared with Mrs. Cooke. As though listening to Mrs. Cooke provide excuses for why Paige would leave without saying goodbye was, somehow, a betrayal of Paige's trust. "Then Jessica and Ian came in talking about how you texted you got a cab to the airport in Concorde, and... well... the rest is a bit of a blur."

Paige thought that 'blur' was probably the most beautiful story ever told by humans. She couldn't wait for the day when she heard every last detail. Right now, however, wasn't the time for details. Eli was here against all odds and in spite of all her lack of belief. The kisses they shared went a long way toward making her more comfortable with her mistake, but she felt she needed verbal confirmation she hadn't burned any shot with him and his daughter all the way to the ground when she left New Hampshire the day before. "I'm sorry I left you and Lucy." Paige felt that foreboding sense of vertigo again. This time it wasn't caused by a kiss, but by a persistent fear of the inevitability of her own loneliness. She had carried that belief with her since she was six years old. Letting go of it was like letting go of her sense of self. It felt terrifying. "If you give me the chance, I will never do it again."

"I believe that." Eli's words were encouragement. She wasn't sure if they were an indication of absolute forgiveness or not.

Did she have the strength to give him the key to her heart? "Eli, I want to tell you something. If after I do, you go running as fast and as far away from me as possible, I want you to know I won't be mad. I will understand."

"Okay."

Eli's face confirmed he couldn't imagine what might follow that bizarre segue. It was helpful, however, as she had painted herself into a corner from which her only hope was to confess. And confess she did. "I love you. I've loved you from the first moment I saw you. The fact that you came all this way to get me tells me I'm not crazy for believing. Am I? Please tell me I'm not David Hume. Please tell me I'm not crazy for believing in the miracle of us."

Paige could tell Eli wasn't sure what David Hume had to do with anything. She could also tell he didn't really care either. "If you're crazy, then call me in love with crazy. I believe we are soulmates. Is that crazy? You tell me. I could ask you to marry me right now. That's how sure I am of what we have. In fact..."

Paige put her finger to his lips just as he was about to bend down on one knee. "Don't do it, Eli. Not because I don't want you to. I do. I mean that." She said it again just so he wouldn't fail to catch the reference. "*I do* want you to. It's just that I am very afraid I will faint if you ask me right now." Paige pointed to her house. "Guess what?"

"What?"

"All my bags are packed and sitting right inside the door of my house. Help me grab them, and then we can get back to the airport, then back to New Hampshire for Christmas." Paige took his hand in hers and led him toward the front door.

"Speaking of the airport." Eli said this with a funny look on his face.

"Yes?" Paige helped him out by providing him with an inflection in her voice that invited clarification.

"We couldn't decide who should come, so we all came." Eli looked as though he thought this was slightly comical now that things had worked out so well.

"You mean you, Lucy, and Jessica?" Paige asked.

"Yes, I mean them. And Ian, and the Cookes, and Vincent." Eli smiled at the memory. "We migrated half the town of Dayton just to make sure you were okay, Paige."

By this point, they were standing on Paige's front porch. Paige fumbled with her keys trying to find the one which unlocked the door. It hit her with devastating precision how loved she was in that moment. The little town in New Hampshire wrapped her in its embrace even before she learned to believe... also as Mr. Wyatt predicted. "I don't know what to say. *Everyone* came?"

"Everyone." Eli looked proud of himself and his town.

The lock finally admitted the key, and Paige opened her door and stepped inside. In the intervening hours since she had last been in her home, the air conditioning far surpassed the warm December. It was too cold in her house now. Paige remembered, without caring about it, that she had never moved the temperature setting back up after she cranked it down when she got home from the airport. She turned to look at Eli. Since she was in the house and he was on the porch, they were closer in height than usual. She was staring almost directly into his eyes. "Eli," she stopped for a moment as the full weight of what she was about to say descended on her, "It's going to be okay, isn't it?"

Eli smiled. "It's going to be much better than okay. It's going to be beautiful."

In her heart, Paige believed.

EPILOGUE

They were in the air and edging toward the East Coast when Christmas Day arrived. Paige, Eli, and Lucy were able to get a row of seats together, and Lucy was snuggled up against her father fast asleep when the clock struck midnight. Eli and Paige were both reading books they had picked up at one of the airport newsstands. Paige noticed the time first. She inclined her book toward her lap, a motion which grabbed Eli's attention. "Merry Christmas," she whispered in his ear.

"Merry Christmas," he answered.

Eli went back to reading his book. Paige leaned her head into the headrest and closed her eyes. She didn't think she would be able to sleep despite the extreme fatigue she felt in all of her body from the dual cases of jetlag. Internally, she smiled to herself as she wondered if jetlag worked the same way positive and negative numbers worked. Would her crisscross of the United States, a six-thousand-mile round trip that clocked in at just under two days, somehow cancel itself out? If the heaviness in her eyelids were any indication, the answer was no.

Paige thought back warmly to the reception she got at LAX from Jessica and all her new friends from Dayton. It was unnerving that they had showed up just for her. She wasn't used to having this much attention paid to her. It felt good though. She would never deny it felt good. Besides, she told herself, it was proper that at least once in a woman's life, the world should stop for her. Paige decided to revel in the glory of her moment. Of the time in her life when the events in her life were worthy of a novel, when she was Mrs. Dalloway. Perhaps she might write it herself. Romance had never been her genre, but maybe it should be. Who knew what the future held for her writing? Now that she believed again, she felt she might attract a much wider audience than the one she knew before. People wanted to hope. They needed to hope. It was the job of the artist to give them ways to do that. No matter what the future held for her writing, she was happy to meet it head-on. She was happy to discover this new version of herself.

Her future with Eli and Lucy fit together in her mind like the plot of a perfect story. She would spend Christmas and New Year's in New Hampshire with them and then fly back and take care of business in Los Angeles. She would resign from her job on the TV show and put her house up for sale. Since it was an affordable, single family home in Los Angeles, it would sell quickly. All of which meant that leaving her West Coast life would be easy.

The flip side, setting up her new life on the East Coast, didn't strike her as that hard either. She and Eli would work out the details together, but she imagined initially she would find a nice place to rent somewhere close to the bed-and-breakfast. Her savings, the proceeds from the sale of her home, and the small income she earned from her four previously published novels would be more than enough to carry her through a year in New Hampshire. She would use the time to work on new writing projects. Stories grounded in belief in things people, like the former Paige Langford, claimed didn't exist.

The only thing unresolved in her mind was the podcast that had been responsible for this whole adventure in the first place. She owed the town of Dayton, and the mayor of Dayton, a Christmas Conversion broadcast. If Lucy agreed, she even had the title of the last show picked out. However, she hadn't had a chance to really talk to Jessica about ending the podcast yet. She wasn't sure how she would respond to pulling the plug on that part of their lives together.

Paige opened her eyes and turned them to Jessica and Ian. They were across the cabin and one row of seats in front of Paige. Jessica had her head resting on Ian's shoulder, and they were both asleep. Paige was forced to smile again. The podcast would work out fine too. If the way Jessica's head fit so comfortably into Ian's shoulder were any indication, Jessica would be moving to New Hampshire right along with Paige. Wouldn't that be a precious Los Angeles ending to their podcasting journey?

§

Paige fell asleep thinking of ways she would repay Mr. Wyatt for the kindness he showed her during her moment of need. If not for his talk at the In-N-Out, who knows what state of mind she would have been in when Eli showed up on her front porch. Mr. Wyatt remained the greatest mystery of all in the way Paige, Eli, and Lucy came together to be a family.

Try as she might through the years which piled up between her Christmas at First Sight and the rest of her life, she never could find him. On the one hand, there was no record of a Henry Wyatt ever living in the house beside hers in Los Angeles. On the other hand, *there was* a Henry Wyatt who had been the mayor of the town of Dayton immediately before Vincent. Paige learned he died, early in the spring of the year of her first Christmas with Eli and Lucy. From Roy at her favorite new used bookstore, she also learned Mr. Wyatt left his collection of books to... Roy. Among those books were the four novels for young adults written by Paige Langford. Those same four books which were later bought by Eli Ryder for his daughter Lucy Ryder.

Many years later when Paige wrote the story of her life, she cast Henry Wyatt, the person who said exactly the right things, at exactly the right moments, as her Christmas Angel.

Call her crazy, but she believed.

THE END

ABOUT THE AUTHOR

Trevor Mccall

Trevor McCall writes sweet, emotionally rich romances that celebrate love, family, and the quiet magic of the holidays. With dozens of heartwarming titles to his name, he's known for crafting stories that feel like a warm mug of cocoa on a snowy evening—comforting, tender, and unforgettable. When he's not writing, Trevor is dreaming up new ways to make readers fall in love with love, one season at a time.

BOOKS BY THIS AUTHOR

First Christmas

Christmas In Trafalgar Square

Christmas In A Bottle

Waiting For Christmas

Christmas Present

Christmas From Scratch

www.ingramcontent.com/pod-product-compliance
Lightning Source LLC
Chambersburg PA
CBHW032118170626
46808CB00006B/1990